Books by J. Frank Dobie

A Vaquero of the Brush Country
Coronado's Children
On the Open Range
Tongues of the Monte
The Flavor of Texas
Apache Gold and Yaqui Silver
John C. Duval: First Texas Man of Letters
The Longhorns
Guide to Life and Literature of the Southwest
A Texan in England
Tales of the Mustang
The Voice of the Coyote
The Ben Lilly Legend
The Mustangs
Tales of Old-Time Texas
I'll Tell You a Tale
Cow People
Rattlesnakes
Some Part of Myself
Out of the Old Rock
Prefaces

PREFACES

J. Frank Dobie

PREFACES

Little, Brown and Company

Boston • Toronto

FIRST EDITION

T 05/75

Acknowledgments for permission to
reprint selections in this book
can be found on pages 201–204.

Library of Congress Cataloging in Publication Data

Dobie, James Frank, 1888–1964.
  Prefaces.

  1. Frontier and pioneer life — The West — Collected works.
  2. The West — History — Collected works.
I. Title.
F591.D62 1975   978   74-34092
ISBN 0-316-18788-7

Designed by D. Christine Benders

*Published simultaneously in Canada
by Little, Brown & Company (Canada) Limited*

PRINTED IN THE UNITED STATES OF AMERICA

Introduction

FRANK DOBIE wrote many prefaces — to a few of his own books; to publications of The Texas Folklore Society, which he edited for many years, and to which he contributed for many more years; and to books written by other people. This book is compiled from forewords written for books by others, some of which were published for the first time and some reprinted. They cover most of Frank's writing career, and so represent changes in style, since he never ceased his effort to "learn to write." It is, however, for another reason that I have thought them worthy to be brought together into a book. Taken as a whole, they establish a theme — the theme of the Old West, which is gone forever.

Two inclusions are prefaces to the work of the artists Charles M. Russell and Frederic Remington and one is to a book of a cartoonist, Jim Williams, one title of whose work, *Out Our Way,* is better known than his own name. Other forewords are concerned with ranchers and their ranches, sheepmen, Indian fighters, and writers about the West. Most are both biographical and critical.

Frank was well aware of the close relationship between a man and the ground he occupied. Upon undertaking a piece of writing, Frank's first move was to visit the land. He expresses this relationship in one of the essays that make up this book, "Belling the Lead Steer":

If somebody could take a sound-recording machine and with about ten miles of film take down all of Jack Potter's tones and drawls and idiomatic phraseology native to the range; if this person could make a life-size painting of him — preferably in the Dutch style — revealing the lust for life that smoulders under his skin and not omitting the chief fang that shows itself while he is chewing tobacco; if, next, this person set down in orderly and plain fashion all that his wonderful memory has stored away on cattle, rattlesnakes, ropes, range men, mirages, drouths, and a thousand other phenomena characteristic of the Southwest, together with the highly intelligent interpretations that the man has given to his penetrating observations — then we should have a picture not only of Jack Potter but of the land to which, root and branch, he belongs; we should have the trail driver breed that he prefigures and the frontier Texan character that he embodies.

The Old West was more than a place; it had its own qualities, as its men had theirs. In the prefaces of this volume many of these qualities appear.

Bertha McKee Dobie

On Waller Creek
Austin, Texas
October 23, 1974

Contents

PREFACES

Andy Adams,
Cowboy Chronicler

FIVE OR SIX YEARS AGO I hunted all over San Antonio
for some books by Andy Adams, and I found just one.
That was one more than the Austin bookstores then had.
A year ago the proprietor of the largest book shop in
Houston assured me that Andy Adams was out of print.
Bookstores of Oklahoma, Kansas, and Boston have proved
as indifferent. Happily, however, the apathy of some of
the book dealers in Texas, particularly in Austin and
Dallas, has been overcome. Now, thanks to an increasingly
large number of individuals who have insisted on the
extraordinary merit of Andy Adams as a writer and as a
historian of the old-time cow people, thousands of his
books are being sold over the Southwest and his delayed
fame is gaining over the entire country. Katharine Fuller-
ton Gerould and Carl Van Doren have during the past
year alluded to him. But the neglect is significant.

The histories of American literature have been singularly silent on him. A contributor to the *Cambridge History of American Literature* mentions him only to show
that he has not read him. Boynton and Haney in their
recent surveys of the field are silent; that considerate
snapper-up of trifles, Fred Lewis Patee, is silent. Several

late authorities, however, mention in one way or another Harold Bell Wright and Zane Grey. Mr. Pattee quotes approvingly somebody's saying that Owen Wister's *The Virginian* is "our last glimpse of the pioneer plainsman and cowboy types, then passing and now gone." By "then" is, I suppose, meant the time at which *The Virginian* appeared; that was 1902. *The Log of a Cowboy* by Andy Adams, his first and perhaps best work, came out in 1903. Following it appeared *A Texas Matchmaker* (1904), *The Outlet* (1905), *Cattle Brands* (1906), *Reed Anthony, Cowman* (1907), and *Wells Brothers* — a book for "boys" — (1911).

The first four books are the best, perhaps, and I should rank them first, second, third, and fourth just as they appeared. Other readers disagree. *The Log of a Cowboy* is the best book that has ever been written of cowboy life, and it is the best book that ever can be written of cowboy life. With its complement, *The Outlet,* it gives a complete picture of trail cattle and trail drivers. Why has it been so overlooked by critics and historians?

In the first place, twenty years ago literary magazines and literary gentlemen were not concerning themselves with the cowboy. Occasionally an article on that subject got into polite print, but honest matter like Charlie Siringo's *A Texas Cowboy* was bound in paper and sold by butcher-boys — a far cry from this day when the Yale University Press publishes James H. Cook's *Fifty Years on the Old Frontier* and then — with a Ph.D. preface — reprints Captain James B. Gillett's *Six Years with the Texas Rangers.* It is true that Owen Wister was at once accepted, but he went west as an Easterner and wrote of the cattle people not as one to the manner born but as a literary connoisseur. Even before him Frederic Remington with *Pony Tracks* and *Crooked Trails* had been accepted into a well-deserved position that he has never lost, but Remington was an artist to whom literature was secondary and to whom the cowboy was tertiary in comparison with Indians and army men. Remington also came into the West looking for local color.

Andy Adams did not come into the cow country looking for "copy." Like Sam Bass, he "was born in Indiana," and again like Sam Bass, "he first came out to Texas a cowboy for to be." He drove the trail as one of the hands. He followed it very much as Conrad and Masefield followed the sea, not as a writer but as a man of the element. The miracle is that when he did write he found such respectable publishers as the Houghton Mifflin Company. He now lives in Colorado Springs, Colorado, aged sixty-six.

Of course, critics not only arouse interest but they follow it, and Mr. Adams, in a letter, attributes neglect of his books to the fact that he "could never make water run uphill or use a fifth wheel," namely a girl. But there is another reason more paradoxical. Generally the development of a particular field by one writer creates a demand for the works of other writers in the same milieu. Unfortunately, however, the demand for cowboy material was first aroused by the "alkali Bill" type of writers; once aroused, that demand has never been satiated, and an avalanche of shoddy has literally buried meritorious writing. Could Andy Adams have led the van, he might have become as well known in his own field as Parkman became known in his. Only just now are responsible readers coming to wonder what the truth about the cowboy is. It is true that twenty years ago *The Log of a Cowboy* was having something of a run and that the newspapers were recording the usual indiscriminating banalities that they record concerning any Western book, but the present attempt at a serious review is just twenty-three years late.

The great virtue of Andy Adams is fidelity, and *The Log of a Cowboy* is a masterpiece for the same reason that *Two Years Before the Mast, Moby Dick,* and *Life on the Mississippi* are masterpieces. All three of these chronicle-records are of the water, and it is "symbolic of something," as Hawthorne would say, that the themes of three of the most faithful expository narratives of America should be offshore.

Now the one part of America that has approached the sea in its length and breadth and dramatic solitude and its elemental power to overwhelm puny man has been the Great Plains. The one phase of American life that has approached the life of a ship's crew alone on the great deep battling the elements has been that of a cow outfit alone on the great trail that stretched across open ranges from Brownsville at the toe of the nation to northwestern Montana and on into Canada. All of Andy Adams's books treat of trail life, except one, *A Texas Matchmaker,* and it treats of ranch life in Southwest Texas during the trail-driving days. I have no hesitancy in saying that Mr. Adams has as truthfully and fully expressed the life of a trail outfit as Dana expressed the life of a crew that sailed around the Horn; that he is as warm in his sympathy for cowmen and horses and cattle as Mark Twain is in his feeling for pilots and the Mississippi River; and that he has treated of

6

cattle as intimately and definitely, though not so scientifi-
cally or dramatically, as Melville treated of whales. Certainly, I have no idea of ranking Andy Adams as the equal
of Mark Twain; I do not believe that he can be ranged
alongside Herman Melville; but I should put him on an
easy level with Richard Henry Dana, Jr. The immense
importance of his subject to the western half of the United
States makes him in a way more important historically
than either Melville or Dana.

Andy Adams has a racy sympathy for the land and for
the cattle and horses and men of the land. He savors them
deep, but he savors them quietly. Sometimes there are
storms and stampedes, but generally the herds just "mosey
along." Cattle bog in the quicksands and there is desperate
work to pull them out, but oftener they graze in the sunshine and chew their cuds by still waters while the owner
rides among them from sheer love of seeing their content-
ment and thriftiness. One old Texas steer took so much
pleasure in hearing the Confederate boys sing "Rock of
Ages" that they could not bear to slaughter him. One trail
outfit made a great pet of a calf, and for hundreds of miles
it followed the chuckwagon, much to the exasperation of
its mother. On another trip there was a certain muley steer
that the horned cattle hooked, and at night the boys used
to let him wander out of the herd to lie down in a private
bed. One spring Reed Anthony, the great cowman, could
not find it in his heart to order a roundup because "chous-
ing" the cattle would disturb the little calves "playing in
groups" and "lying like fawns in the tall grass." "The
Story of a Poker Steer" in *Cattle Brands* is a classic; its
delineation of the life of a "linebacked calf" is as quiet and

easy as Kipling's "Story of the White Seal." Tom Quirk, boarding a train in Montana, thousands of miles away from his Texas home, was grieved indeed to part from his saddle horse forever.

No matter whether the theme is a pet calf or a terrible "die-up" in "the Territory," there is absolutely no strain in Andy Adams. This quality of reserve distinguishes him from all other Western writers that I know of. One can but contrast him with the Zane Grey school so ubiquitously exploited by nearly every American institution ranging from a two-bit drugstore to Harper and Brothers. In Zane Grey's *U. P. Trail,* for instance, which has often been hailed as a piece of real history, the men "were grim; they were indomitable"; and the heroine "clutched Neal with fingers of steel, in a grip that he could not have loosened without breaking her bones."

Not long ago a friend was telling me of an incident so expressive that I must repeat it. This friend was camping in a canyon out in Arizona, where he was excavating some Indian ruins. One night he was awakened by unearthly yelling and shooting and the clatter of horses' hoofs. Rushing out of his tent, he met a cowboy whom he knew. "What is the matter?" he asked. "Oh," replied the cowboy, "there's a feller coming back yonder who hired us to give him some local color, as he calls it. His name's Zane Grey, and we're doing our damndest to give him all the hell he calls for."

Now in Andy Adams always "there is ample time," as he makes "a true Texan" say. To quote the words of Gilbert Chesterton on Sir Walter Scott's heroes, "the men linger long at their meals." Indeed, I think that the best things in the books of Mr. Adams are the tales that the men tell around the chuckwagon and the jokes and the chaff that they indulge in there.

An easy intimacy with the life shows on every page. The man writes of the only life he knows, in the only language he knows. "Now, Miller, the foreman, hadn't any use for a man that wasn't dead tough under any condition. I've known him to camp his outfit on alkali water, so the men would get out in the morning, and every rascal beg leave to ride outside circle on the morning round-up." "Cattle will not graze freely in a heavy dew or too early in the morning." When Don Lovell's outfit received a herd of cattle on the Rio Grande, the Texas boss tallied the hundreds with a tally string and the Mexican caporal tallied them by dropping pebbles from one hand to the other. When June Deweese, *segundo,* showed off his boss's horses to a buyer below San Antonio, he had them grazing on a hillside and drove the buyer along on the lower slope so that they would appear larger.

The language that the Andy Adams cowboys use is as natural and honest as the exposition; it is often picturesque, too, as all language of the soil is. I quote sentences almost at random from various of the books. "I'll build a fire in your face that you can read the San Francisco 'Examiner' by at midnight." "We had the outfits and the horses, and our men were plainsmen and were at home as long as they could see the north star." "The old lady was bogged to the saddle skirts in her story." "Blankets? Never use them; sleep on your belly and cover with your back, and get up with the birds in the morning." "Every good cowman takes his saddle wherever he goes, though he may not have clothes enough to dust a fiddle."

A year or so ago in a senseless attack on the historical accuracy of Emerson Hough's *North of Thirty-Six,* Stuart Henry said that the Texans who reached Abilene in 1867 did not celebrate the Fourth of July. The charge, along with others, was repudiated by some good Texas Americans. Now, as a matter of fact, it is very likely that the Texans of 1867 did not celebrate the Fourth of July in Abilene or anywhere else. I know a few — and they are out of the old rock, too — who still pay more attention to April 21 than to July 4. During the three decades following the Civil War more than ten millions of cattle were trailed north from Texas; they were trailed across every river and into every range of the West, and wherever they were trailed the pointmen were Texans. Generally those Texans were either Confederate soldiers or the sons of Confederate soldiers. Andy Adams has been very careful to catch the temper of those Texans fresh from the ranks of the Confederate Army. He has not allowed, like other writers, a mushy patriotism to abnegate the justified pride of a section, though in his books the halest of partnerships are formed between "rebels" and Yankees. In 1882, at Frenchman's Ford on the Yellowstone, "The Rebel," a memorable hand in *The Log of a Cowboy,* exulted over a "patriotic beauty" with a toast that went thus: "Jeff Davis and the Southern Confederacy."

When I began reading Andy Adams a number of years ago, the humor of his books did not impress me. Lately I have found it to be one of their highest virtues. Folk yarns salt page after page, and many a good-natured drawl sets me laughing. The humor is as unconscious as the green of grass, but I do not know of anything in Mark Twain funnier than the long story of the "chuckline rider" who blew into a cow camp in "The Strip" about Christmas time and proceeded to earn his board by cooking "bear sign" (the name for doughnuts). The cowboys often play like colts; one of them gets down off his horse and butts his head into a muddy bank, imitative of the cattle; some of them dress up one of their number like a wild Indian and take him to the hotel for dinner. This is horseplay, to be sure, but as it is told it generates health in a healthy reader like a good feed of roast beef and plum pudding.

There are, of course, many shortcomings in Mr. Adams. His books have no plots, but lack of plot sometimes allows of an easier fidelity to facts. He lacks great dramatic power, unless the quiet truth be dramatic. However, there is plenty of action on occasion. "The men of that day," says the author of *Reed Anthony, Cowman,* which like all the other novels but one is written in the autobiographic style, "were willing to back their opinions, even on trivial matters, with their lives. 'I'm the quickest man on the trigger that ever came over the trail,' said a cow puncher to me one night in a saloon in Abilene. 'You're a blankety blank liar,' said a quiet little man, a perfect stranger to both of us, not even casting a glance our way. I wrested a six-shooter from the hands of my acquaintance, and hustled him out of the house, getting roundly cursed for my interference, though no doubt I saved human life."

The greatest shortcoming, perhaps, is too much love of prosperity. Andy Adams loves cowmen and cattle and horses so that he can hardly suffer any of them to undergo

11

ruin. The trail has hardships, but it is delightful. The path of the owner and his cowboys is sometimes rocky, but it generally leads down into pleasant pastures. As they travel it, they never go into heroics about their "grim sacrifices," etc.; they take great gusto in the traveling. When I read *Reed Anthony, Cowman* or *Wells Brothers,* I think of old Daniel Defoe's love for goods of the earth, and I would no more think of holding their prosperity against the actuality of Reed Anthony, Don Lovell, and other prosperous cattle people of Andy Adams's creation than I would think of impeaching the life-likeness of Mulberry Sellers on account of his optimism.

There are no women in Andy Adams, excepting those in the melancholy *Matchmaker.* Well, there were no women in the action that he treats of. Why should he lug them in? Nor has Andy Adams any thesis to advance. He has no absorbing philosophy of life that mingles with the dark elements of earth as in Joseph Conrad. "To those who love them, cattle and horses are good company." Perhaps that is his philosophy.

It is easy to let one's enthusiasm run away with one's judgment. I have waited a long time to write these words on Andy Adams. Perhaps sympathy for his subject has biased me. Perhaps the memory of how a dear uncle of mine used to "run" with him at the end of the trail in Caldwell, Kansas, has affected me. I try to rule those elements out. It is my firm conviction that one hundred, three hundred years from now people will read Andy Adams to see what the life of those men who went up the trail from Texas was like, just as we now read the diary of Pepys to see what life in London was like following the Restoration, or as we read the *Spectator* papers to see what it was like in the Augustan age. Those readers of other centuries will miss in Andy Adams the fine art of Addison, though they will find something of the same serenity; they will miss the complex character and debonair judgments of Pepys; but they will find the honesty and fidelity of a man who rode his horses straight without giving them the sore-back and then who traced his trail so plainly that even a tenderfoot may follow it without getting lost.

Foreword to "A Texas Ranger," by Napoleon Augustus Jennings

". . . BROUGHT IN THE BODY of Pedro Paralis, a noted cow thief. He resisted arrest and died with a dozen bullet holes through him."

Thus reads the postscript to a letter signed "very respectfully" by L. H. McNelly, captain of an independent company of Texas rangers, dated at Brownsville, December 5, 1875, addressed to his adjutant general, and now with other reports similarly laconic preserved in the state archives at Austin.

Although that postscript, representative in its nakedness, may be regarded as an item of history, from such materials alone a history that makes the past live could never be written. And if any time of the past was ever vivid and vital enough to live on through mere reporting — reporting without adornment or other adventitious trappings — it was the time when McNelly's rangers rode the bloody border of Texas. Hence it is exceedingly fortunate that a man who was to become a skilled reporter rode with them and later saw reason for putting down some of the things he had been a part of.*

---

* For biographical material in the sketch that follows I am indebted to the widow of N. A. Jennings, Madam Edith Helena, Purdy Station, New York.

Napoleon Augustus Jennings was born in Philadelphia, January 11, 1856. Most of his boyhood was spent at St. Paul's School in Concord, New Hampshire. Of the literature that he read and the motives that brought him to Texas at the age of eighteen, he has himself told. What happened to him during the next four years is a part of *A Texas Ranger*.

The death of his father in 1878 took him back to Philadelphia, where his family hoped that he would settle down to business. But the city seemed literally to smother him. Again he turned to the open ranges, this time in the Far West. He rode as a cowboy; he drove a mountain stage; he prospected and mined; he painted signs and did other things. Again he returned to Philadelphia, to enter now on the profession that he was to die in, that of a newspaper man.

In 1884, at the age of twenty-eight, having already lived more positive days than most men live during a lifetime, he began work on the Philadelphia *News,* switched successively to the *Times* and *Tribune* of that city, next to the New York *Star,* and then, in 1887, to the *Sun,* which the genius of Charles A. Dana had made the lodestar of every ambitious reporter in America. Five years later he found himself on the staff of the San Antonio *Express* — a position that brought him again in contact with Texas rangers. Two years later he settled down for a long term with the New York *Evening World.* His fiery verses printed in newspapers during the Spanish-American War won him the title of "the *automatic* poet." Meantime he had begun writing for the *Youth's Companion,* the *Saturday Evening Post,* and other magazines. He wrote anecdotes, for he was a fecund raconteur. He wrote stories of adventure, some of them designed especially for boys (like one printed in *St. Nicholas*) and all of them suitable for boys; the titles of two that appeared in the *Saturday Evening Post*, "A Dash for the Border" and "La Ley de Fuga," almost tell the story. He wrote biographical sketches; and one of them, "Lee Hall," about the famous Texas ranger who so influenced O. Henry, should be preserved. It appeared in the *Saturday Evening Post*, January 6, 1900.

Anecdotes of his facility as a reporter — and this is a striking quality in *A Texas Ranger* — yet linger. One night he was sent to interview Mark Twain. Other reporters presented themselves for the same purpose. But the great humorist was ill — very, very ill. He couldn't think of anything to say even if he felt like talking. Then Jennings asked if he might write an interview anyhow. "Go ahead, Jennings," Mark Twain replied, "for I am positive you wouldn't write anything I wouldn't say." The interview, which appeared in the New York *Evening World* next day, told how Mark Twain told about the cat that sat on the red-hot stove lid — and the yarn is still repeated as one of Mark Twain's "characteristic" clinchings of a bit of philosophy.

While Roosevelt was police commissioner of the city of New York, Jennings had satirized him, but the career of the Rough Rider changed the journalist into an admirer and the two men became good friends. Indeed, during Roosevelt's race for the governorship Jennings acted as his publicity agent.

During the first decade of the century Jennings toured Europe and the United States as press agent and manager for his wife, Madam Edith Helena, operatic and vaudeville singer. The Madero Revolution, however, was too good for him to miss, and in 1910 he went to Mexico City on the *Herald* staff. During the World War his energies, like Roosevelt's, flared up once more — into words. He died December 15, 1919, in New York City.

Jennings belonged to the age of Roosevelt and Richard Harding Davis, and although he did not attain anything like an eminence comparable to that attained by either of those life-loving celebrities, it is hardly too much to say that the Strenuous One never wrote a history nor the great war correspondent a romance surpassing in sheer readableness *A Texas Ranger*. It appeared in 1899 with the imprint of Charles Scribner's Sons. Once, upon being asked why he had written it, Jennings replied: "I am a writing man; I needed money; I had a story to tell; I told it." Why the book has been allowed to run out of print is a puzzle; but why during recent years copies when available should have brought twenty-five or thirty dollars is not hard to explain. I defy anyone to read it without being engaged by its brightness and ranger-swift directness. The swing of young men in the saddle runs through the pages.

> Then mount and away! give the fleet steed the rein;
> The ranger's at home on the prairies again.

Is the book true? The question is bound to be asked. The available muster rolls of McNelly's ranger company, which are by no means complete, show that N. A. Jennings certainly served from May 26, 1876, to February 1, 1877. In a letter written from New York City, dated July 7,

1899, to the widow of Captain McNelly (who married W. T. Wroe and now lives in Austin), Jennings comments on his newly published work thus: "In the book I made myself a member of the company a year before I actually joined. I did this to add interest to the recital and to avoid too much of a hear-say character. Told in the first person adventures hold the attention of the reader much more closely than at second hand."

Jennings himself, then, was not along when in June, 1875, "the McNelly men" laid out on the plaza in Brownsville — for whoever wanted to claim them — the bodies of thirteen Mexican bandits they had "naturalized"; nor was he, later on in the same year, with McNelly when that daring leader defied the United States government, crossed the Rio Grande, and fought the Cortina raiders at Las Cuevas. Nevertheless, joining this extraordinary body of men some months later, Jennings scouted with them long enough to absorb their technique, their traditions, their spirit. If his own eyes did not see every act he has described, we may yet be sure that the stuff of his book, which is only incidentally autobiography, came to him from eyewitnesses. He probably telescoped some events; space and the exigencies of narrative necessarily prevented his giving credit to every individual ranger who took part in the exploits recorded. Every writer who expects to be read must be selective, and many a historian who wanted to make the truth live has buried it in a dismal swamp of unselected facts.

Once I asked S. N. Hardy, a former McNelly ranger who served along with Jennings, this question:

"Did Jennings exaggerate the lawless conditions on the border in the seventies?"

"No," he replied, "it would be impossible to exaggerate the conditions. Why, when Dimmitt County — a part of the region where King Fisher's outlaws operated — was organized in 1880, only one man among the first set of county officials had not killed a man. That, though, does not mean they were bad men."

Then the veteran went on to relate an incident connected with Jesus Sandoval, the singular Mexican ranger whom Jennings describes so graphically in Chapter Ten. "One night while we were camped on the Rio Grande," Ranger Hardy relates, "I was in charge of the guard. Sandoval was keeping watch, and along about midnight I heard him cursing a blue streak in both Mexican and English. I went down to see what the trouble was. When I got near the river I saw an empty skiff, which had come over from the Mexican side. Also I saw Sandoval on his horse riding against a taut rope that was hitched to his saddle horn. The other end of the rope was tied to the neck of a Mexican. The Mexican's feet were tied to a mesquite bush. After Sandoval got through pulling, he dismounted and showed me another Mexican whose throat had been cut to the neckbone. He then explained that these two victims were the last of the gang who had burned his home and ruined his wife and daughter. I did not say anything about the matter to Captain McNelly until months later. Lots of things happened on the Rio Grande that never got into the ranger reports."

Down in the brush country between the Nueces River and the Rio Bravo the tradition of McNelly's rangers is a part of the inheritance of the soil. Some of the people think that McNelly won the battle of San Jacinto! From what men who knew him say, McNelly was "hard." He made many a meal off nothing but mesquite beans. He slept many a night with nothing but a saddle blanket to protect him against mud and cold rain. He seldom, if ever, praised a man under him. If a man could not stand the gaff, was unfit to keep the pace, did not live up to the code, then he was discharged, usually "dishonorably." McNelly had little patience with failure to get an outlaw because of caution. At the same time he saw little use of risking a good ranger's life to arrest a moronic bad man — and a majority of the bad men were mental as well as moral degenerates — only to see him later released by an intimidated jury. Yet it was his duty to rid the country of the cutthroat element. There was a way. "Take no chances," he once said to Sergeant Armstrong. "Chance" was sometimes a synonym for "prisoner." On this particular occasion Armstrong and his detail of rangers took no chances; as a result either five or eight — authorities vary as to the number — outlaws awoke in the dead of night in their camp beside the Espantosa Lake to bite the dust. Regardless of the number, the riddance was good and was necessary to be accomplished in the way it was accomplished.

Yes, McNelly was a hard man — with outlaws. He lived in hard times. He had also the blood of Virginia chivalry in his veins. It is strange that a ranger and a gentleman in combination should be considered contradictory while "a soldier and a gentleman" is a commonplace. Let people who cannot understand the combination in "a ranger and a gentleman" read a little pamphlet written by Mrs. D. W.

Roberts, wife of a ranger captain, on her experiences in a ranger camp. Let people who flinch at the idea of goriness and courtesy combined in a ranger read the lives "gay and gore" of such gallants as Sir Francis Drake. The rangers of Jennings's time were as a rule anything but ruffians, even though many of them had had their training on the frontier. They were hand-picked men, and a well-bred youngster like Jennings was at home among them. They loved living.

When at the age of thirty-one, on September 4, 1877, L. H. McNelly, the intrepid ranger, died, the disease which took him off having been brought on by exposure in the line of duty, he was buried in the village of Burton in Washington County, Texas, and Captain Richard King, representing the ranchmen of the border ranges, erected there a granite monument to his memory. It was a decent memorial, but it was not needed to keep the McNelly name green.

Although, like "cowboy," the word "ranger" was old long before English-speaking colonists crossed the Mississippi River, it remained for Texas to give both words the connotations they now bear. The body of writings connected with cowboys has grown to be rather voluminous. Cowboys rode from the Sierra Madre to the prairies of Alberta, from the coast of Oregon to the eastern sweep of the Gulf of Mexico; they numbered thousands upon thousands. The Texas rangers never numbered above a few hundred at one time, as a usual thing not above a few score. Their range, wide as it was, was yet confined to the territory of the state they served. Considering their proud and far-flung reputation, the literature about them is ex-

21

ceedingly limited; a thorough history of the corps is yet to be written. It is a matter for genuine gratulation that, along with James B. Gillett's excellent *Six Years with the Texas Rangers*, Jennings's *A Texas Ranger* is now made available for boys and men and women who like a brave, clean-cut narrative, simply and honestly told, about those brave and clean-cut frontiersmen, the Texas rangers.

Austin, Texas
San Jacinto Day, 1930

A Preface on
Authentic Liars

AN AUTHENTIC LIAR knows what he is lying about, knows that his listeners — unless they are tenderfeet, greenhorns — know also, and hence makes no pretense of fooling either himself or them. At his best he is as grave as a historian of the Roman Empire; yet what he is after is neither credulity nor the establishment of truth. He does not take himself too seriously, but he does regard himself as an artist and yearns for recognition of his art. He may lie with satiric intent; he may lie merely to make the time pass pleasantly; he may lie in order to take the wind out of some egotistic fellow of his own tribe or to take in some greener; again, without any purpose at all and directed only by his ebullient and companion-loving nature, he may "stretch the blanket" merely because, like the redoubtable Tom Ochiltree, he had "rather lie on credit than tell truth for cash." His generous nature revolts at the monotony of everyday facts and overflows with desire to make his company joyful.

Certainly the telling of "windies" flourished in the Old World long before America was discovered; nevertheless the tall tale both in subject matter and in manner of telling has been peculiar to the frontiers of America, whether in the backwoods of the Old South, in the mining camps of the Far West, amid the logging camps presided over by Paul Bunyan, or on the range lands stretching from the Gulf of Mexico to the Canadian line. Very likely the Pilgrim Fathers did not indulge much in the art of yarning, and the stately Cavaliers pretty much left that sort of entertainment to the poor — "poor but honest" — settlers. As to whether the "decay in the art of lying" that Oscar Wilde observed in literary fiction has blighted that to be heard around campfires and on the galleries of ranch houses, we need not here inquire. The "big uns" that Mody Boatright has gathered together in this book are not altogether out of the past.

They express a way that range folk talked and they express also a way in which these folk cartooned objects familiar to them like rattlesnakes, sandstorms, jackrabbits, the expanding and contracting powers of rawhide, the suddenness of Texas northers, "killings" according to a code that clearly distinguished a killing from a murder, and other things. They are, in short, authentic both as to the characters represented and the subjects discoursed upon.

When in the old days two cow outfits met upon the range, and there was "ample time," as Andy Adams would say, they sometimes arranged what was known as an "auguring match." Each outfit would pit its prime yarn-spinner against the other's and there followed a contest not only of invention but of endurance. John Palliser in *The Solitary Hunter; or, Sporting Adventures of the Prairies* (London, 1856) relates how after an all-night talking contest between a Missourian and a Kentuckian, the umpire "at a quarter past five" found the Kentucky man fast asleep, his opponent "sitting up close beside him and whispering in his ear." What the contestants talked about, Palliser does not say, but there is ample testimony to prove that the "auguring matches" on the range had a precedent among the backwoodsmen of the South who were to push out upon the ranges a kind of round-table talk in which each talker sought to cap the tall tales of his fellow with one a little taller.

For genuine artists a solitary opponent is sufficient; art is substantive. In *Piney Woods Tavern; or, Sam Slick in Texas* (Philadelphia, 1858), by Samuel A. Hammett, the narrator in traveling from the Brazos to the Trinity rivers found the San Jacinto "a roarin' and a hummin' it. . . . Free soil movements was a-goin' on, and trees a-tumblin' in all along the banks."

I see thar war no help for it [the narrator goes on]. So I took my feet outen the stirrups, threw my saddle-bags over my shoulder, and in me and the mare went.

We war in a awful tight place for a time, but we soon landed safe. I'd jest got my critter tied out, and a fire started to dry myself with when I see a chap come ridin' up the hill on a smart chunk of a pony. . . .

"Hoopee! stranger" — sings out my beauty — "How d'ye? Kept your fireworks dry, eh? How in thunder did ye get over?"

"Oh!" says I, "mighty easy. Ye see, stranger, I'm powerful on a pirogue; so I waited till I see a big log a-driftin' nigh the shore, when I fastened to it, set my critter a-straddle on it, got into the saddle, paddled over with my saddle-bags, and steered with the mare's tail."

"Ye didn't, though, by Ned!" says he, "did ye?"

"Mighty apt to" — says I — "but arter ye've sucked all that in and got yer breath agin, let's know how *you* crossed?"

"Oh!" says he, settin' his pig's eyes on me. "I've been a-riding all day with a consarned ager, and orful dry, and afeard to drink at the prairie water holes; so when I got to the river I jest went in fer a big drink, swallered half a mile of water, and come over dry shod."

"Stranger," says I, "ye'r just one huckleberry above my persimmon. Light and take some red-eye. I thought ye looked green, but I were barkin' up the wrong tree."

Storytelling in Texas was so popular that at times it interfered with religion. The pioneer Baptist preacher Z. N. Morrell relates in his autobiographic *Flowers and Fruits in the Wilderness* (Dallas, 1886) that on one occasion while he was preaching in a log cabin in East Texas his sermon was drowned by the voices of men outside "telling anecdotes." After an ineffectual reprimand, the preacher finally told his interrupters that if they would give him a chance he would tell an anecdote and that then, if it was not better than any of theirs, he would "take down his sign and listen to them." They agreed to the challenge. The anecdote he proceeded to relate about Sam Houston and the battle of San Jacinto won him the right to keep on talking without interruption. The triumph was but a repetition of David Crockett's election to Congress through his b'ar stories.

An anecdote is not by any means necessarily a windy, but people who cultivate the art of oral narration will sooner or later indulge in exaggerative invention. Some candidate for the Ph.D. degree should write a thesis on the interrelationship of the anecdote, the tall tale, and the short story in America. What is probably the most widely

known story that the nation has produced, "The Celebrated Jumping Frog of Calaveras County," is all three —
and it is mostly just a yarn in which the frontier character
Jim Smiley, character being the essence of good anecdote,
is more important than the frog.

Sixty years or so ago at Covey's college for ranch boys,
located at Concrete, Texas, near Cuero, the "scholars"
organized a liar's club. According to the rules of the club
every boy present at a session must tell a story. The teller
of what was adjudged the best yarn was habitually awarded
as prize a dozen hot tamales cooked by one of the Mexican
women about the premises.

One night a certain lad of few words who had been
drawn into the club was called upon to contribute.

"Wall," he drawled, "I was raised away out in the bresh
up whur I never heared nobody talk, and I jes' ain't got
no story to tell."

"Oh, go on and tell something," the other club members
urged.

"No," the diffident youth remonstrated, "it ain't no use
fer me to try to make up anything. I jest can't do it. I've
been a-trying to figger up something while you all was
telling your stories, and the pump won't even prime."

There was more urging and encouraging. But still the
boy from up the creek hung back. As a member of the
club, however, he simply had to tell something — or "take
the leggins." Finally the leader of the group suggested, "I
guess we can let you off from lying if you're so much like
George Washington. Just go ahead and tell us about some
interesting happening. It don't have to be a lie."

"Wall," the drawly tongue started off, "I'll tell you

27

about something that happened to me. One morning I was
a-leaving the ranch to look out for wormy calves. I was
going to be gone all day, and jest as I throwed my leg over
the saddle, a Meskin girl that lived with her people in a
jacal close to the corral came a-running out. 'Here,' says
she, 'we've jest been making tamales out of the cow that
got her leg broke yesterday and you all had to kill. The
meat is fat and the corn is new, and the tamales are *muy
sabroso.* You must take some of them with you.'

"Now I would do nearly anything this little Meskin girl
suggested. So I told her all right, to wrop the tamales up
in some paper and a flour sack and I'd put 'em in my
morral with the hank of dried beef and the bottle of worm
medicine. Which she did. Tamales ain't much good unless
they are hot, you know, and I figgered the wropping would
keep these warm.

"Well, after I'd gone about six miles, I struck a bull that
I decided to rope. Which I did. The bull he kept on going
after he hit the end of the rope and my horse he could not
stop him. He dragged me about forty miles more or less,
I guess, before I hung up in a mesquite tree with my chin
between the forks of a limb. I don't know how long I hung
there, but it was some time. People differ as to how long it
was. Anyway, it was until the limb rotted down and I
dropped to the ground.

"I didn't want to go back to the ranch afoot, and so I
hit out follering the horse's tracks. I found him a good
piece out looking purty gant but still saddled and the rope
that had rotted off the bull's neck still tied to the horn of
the saddle. I went right up to the morral, for it was still
on the saddle, and untied it. I was a little gant myself.

28

Then I felt of the sacking around the tamales, and I couldn't feel no heat. Says I to myself, 'I bet that Meskin girl didn't wrop 'em right and the danged things have got so cold they won't be no count to eat.' But I went on and unwropped the paper, and when I got to the shucks, danged if they didn't burn my fingers. Them tamales shore tasted good after all that bull running and then hoofing it after the horse. It is remarkable the way tamales hold the heat when they are well wropped."

Even the schools for ranch boys in Texas included "windjamming" among their activities. But many a frontiersman who had not had the advantage of an education must have been forced by circumstances to "make it strong" in telling about the Wild West to gentle Easterners. Every new land has marvels; hence "traveler's tales." When facts are taken for fabrications, then the narrator is tempted to "cut loose" sure enough. One of the most honest-hearted and reliable frontiersmen that ever boiled coffee over mesquite coals was Bigfoot Wallace. He came to Texas from Virginia long before barbed wire "played hell" with the longhorns. After he had himself become a regular Longhorn he went back to his old home for a visit. As John C. Duval in the delightful *Adventures of Bigfoot Wallace* (1870) has the old frontiersman describe his reception, he was egged on in the following manner to take the bridle off and let out the last kink.

A few weeks after my arrival I went to a fandango that was given for my special benefit. There was a great crowd there, and everybody was anxious to see the "Wild Texan," as they called me. I was the lion of the evening, particularly for the young ladies, who never tired of asking me questions about Mexico, Texas, the Indians, prairies, etc. I at first answered truthfully all the questions they asked me; but when I found they evidently doubted some of the stories I told them which were facts, then I branched out and gave them some whoppers. These they swallowed down without gagging. For instance, one young woman wanted to know how many wild horses I had ever seen in a drove. I told her perhaps thirty or forty thousand.

"Oh, now! Mr. Wallace," said she, "don't try to make game of me in that way. Forty thousand horses in one drove! Well, I declare you are a second Munchausen!"*

"Well, then," said I, "maybe you won't believe me when I tell you there is a sort of spider in Texas as big as a peck measure, the bite of which can only be cured by music."

"Oh, yes," she answered, "I believe that's all so, for I have read about them in a book."

Among other whoppers, I told her there was a varmint in Texas called the Santa Fe, that was still worse than the tarantula, for the best brass band in the country couldn't cure their sting; that the creatures had a hundred legs and a sting on every one of them, besides two large stings in its forked tail, and fangs as big as a rattlesnake's. When they sting you with their legs alone, you might possibly live an hour; when with all their stings, perhaps fifteen or twenty minutes; but when they sting and bite you at the same time, you first turn blue, then yellow, and then a beautiful bottle-green, when your hair all falls out, and your finger nails drop off, and in five minutes you are as dead as a door nail, in spite of all the doctors in America.

---

* Forty thousand, even thirty thousand, mustangs are a lot of mustangs. In *The Young Explorers,* a book privately printed in Austin, Texas, about 1892, Duval, pp. 111–112, defends this extraordinary assertion. The wild horses were encountered between the Nueces River and the Rio Grande. Corroborative of the enormous numbers to be found in that region is the testimony of William A. McClintock, "Journal of a Trip Through Texas and Northern Mexico," *Southwestern Historical Quarterly,* Vol. XXXIV, pp. 232–233. Bigfoot Wallace was not lying about the wild horses.

"Oh! My! Mr. Wallace!" said she. "How have you managed to live so long in that horrible country?"

"Why, you see," said I, "with my tarantula boots made of alligator skin, and my centipede hunting-shirt made of tanned rattlesnake hides, I have escaped pretty well; but these don't protect you against the stinging scorpions, cow-killers, and scaly-back chinches, that crawl about at night when you are asleep! The only way to keep them at a distance is to chaw tobacco and drink whiskey, and that is the reason the Temperance Society never flourished much in Texas."

"Oh!" said she, "what a horrible country that must be, where the people have to be stung to death, or else chaw tobacco and drink whiskey! I don't know which is the worst."

"Well," said I, "the people out there don't seem to mind it much; they get used to it after a while. In fact, they seem rather to like it, for they chaw tobacco and drink whiskey even in the winter time, when the cow-killers and stinging lizards are all frozen up!"

What gusto, what warmth of natural sympathy, what genial expansion! Here the authentic liar has been translated by circumstances and by his own genius into the pure aura of truth. There is no distortion, no "wrenching the true cause the wrong way," no base intent to win by arousing false fears or to defraud through false hopes. The artist has but arranged the objects of his scene and then handed the spectator a magnifying glass that is flawlessly translucent. The magnified vision, like that of Tartarin of Tarascon, seems but the effect of a sunlight transilluminating all other sunlights — the sunlight of Tartarin's Midi country, "the only liar in the Midi." Only here it is the sunlight of the West, which brings mountain ranges a hundred miles away within apparent touching distance and through its mirages makes antelopes stalk as tall as giraffes, gives to buffalo bulls far out on the prairies the proportions of haywagons, and reveals spired cities and tree-shadowed lakes reposing in deserts actually so devoid of life that not even a single blade of green grass can there be found.

Occasionally one of these authentic liars of the West falls a prey to his own lying. Frank Root (*The Overland Stage to California*) relates that one time after a Gargantuan storyteller named Ranger Jones had finished narrating a particularly blood-curdling "personal experience," a stage driver who happened to be among the listeners looked him squarely in the eye and said, "I hope, Ranger Jones, that you don't expect me to believe this story."

"Well — er — no — really, I don't," the narrator answered. "The fact is, I have lied out here in this Western country so long and have been in the habit of telling so many damned lies, the truth of it is now that I don't know when I can believe myself." In *Trails Plowed Under* Charles M. Russell has a delicious chapter on "Some Liars of the Old West."

"These men weren't vicious liars," he comments. "It was love of romance, lack of reading matter, and the wish to be entertainin' that makes 'em stretch facts and invent yarns." Among the most famous of these liars was a man known as Lyin' Jack, and his favorite tale was on an elk he once killed that had a spread of antlers fifteen feet wide. He always kept these, as he told the story, in the loft of his cabin.

One time after a long absence Lyin' Jack showed up in Benton. "The boys" were all glad to see him and, after a round or two of drinks, asked him for a yarn.

32

"No, boys," said Jack, "I'm through. For years I've been tellin' these lies — told 'em so often I got to believin' 'em myself. That story of mine about the elk with the fifteen-foot horns is what cured me. I told about that elk so often that I knowed the place I killed it. One night I lit a candle and crawled up in the loft to view the horns — an' I'm damned if they weren't there."

In a book of not enough consequence to warrant the naming of its title, the author, writing through hearsay and attempting to be veracious, describes the Texas norther — which comes "sudden and soon in the dead of night or the blaze of noon" — as being so swift in descent, so terrible in force, and so bitterly cold that "no old Texan would trust himself out on the prairies in July or August with the thermometer at ninety-six degrees, without two blankets strapped at the saddle-bow to keep him from freezing to death should a norther blow up." Of course no man of the range carries his blankets on the horn of a saddle and no Texan ever experienced a genuine norther in July or August. The description is utterly false, utterly lacking in authenticity. On the other hand, when "Mr. Fishback of the Sulphurs" relates how one hot day in December when he was riding home he saw a blue norther coming behind him, put spurs to his horse, and, racing for miles with the nose of the wind at his very backbone, arrived at the stable to find the hindquarters of his horse frozen stiff whereas the forequarters were in a lather of sweat — such a hair's breadth doth divide the hot prelude to a norther from the iciness of the norther itself — we realize that we are in the company of a liar as authentic as he is accomplished. Surely such do not violate the ninth commandment; indeed they have become as little children.

Austin, Texas
Cinco de Mayo, 1934

Belling the Lead Steer

THE MEXICAN VAQUEROS used to call Jack Potter "Meester Yaqui," and Yaqui is what I call him. That "Colonel" business betrays him. He is a good enough Indian to deserve the name, and he's a tribesman from who laid the chunk. If somebody could take a sound-recording machine and with about ten miles of film take down all of Jack Potter's tones and drawls and idiomatic phraseology native to the range; if this person could make a life-size painting of him — preferably in the Dutch style — revealing the lust for life that smoulders under his skin and not omitting the chief fang that shows itself while he is chewing tobacco; if, next, this person set down in orderly and plain fashion all that his wonderful memory has stored away on cattle, rattlesnakes, ropes, range men, mirages, drouths, and a thousand other phenomena characteristic of the Southwest, together with the highly intelligent interpretations that the man has given to his penetrating observations — then we should have a picture not only of Jack Potter but of the land to which, root and branch, he belongs; we should have the trail driver breed that he prefigures and the frontier Texan character that he embodies.

"I'm strong on the breed," as the chuckwagon philosopher in Andy Adams's *The Log of a Cowboy* says, explaining why he did not marry a girl belonging to a family of "razorback, barnyard savages." Anybody who knows anything about horses and cows has to be strong on the breed, and when I see a pair of human morons imagining that their offsprings may turn out to be a second George Washington or Florence Nightingale, I merely recognize further evidence of the moronic quality. I know that Jack Potter's mother must have been a strong character; his father even in life became a tradition. Yaqui is a true chip off the old block.

This father, Andrew Jackson Potter, was known as the Fighting Parson. He had been a roving gambler. Any day he wants to listen, a person in Southwest Texas can hear stories about Parson Potter. He rode his circuits at a time when a gun was much more essential to a man's wardrobe than a pair of pajamas. (I'd be willing to bet that Jack Potter has not learned to wear pajamas yet.) The use of this gun was not necessarily confined to Indians.

One time when Parson Potter had an engagement to preach at Hondo, he was warned by friends that two rowdies had been in the habit of breaking up services attempted there. When Potter entered the room to take his place before the improvised pulpit, he had his Bible in one hand and Old Betsy in the other. He laid Old Betsy across the pulpit. Then he stood up and announced that if anybody present objected to his preaching, he would attend to the objections after the services but that they had better not be voiced during the services. The rowdies were present. They kept silent not only all through the services but afterwards.

Parson Potter knew all kinds of men, and his genial nature made him a favorite with characters in some ways his opposite. For instance, as a story goes, Parson Potter, after having preached to a congregation at San Angelo in which men were conspicuous for their absence, entered a saloon. It was swarming with men. He had a great carrying voice, and now he boomed out, "Why, I was thinking all the women in this town were widows. I see they're not. I believe I'll preach here right now and give the men a chance to listen." Immediately a billiard table was cleared for him to occupy as a rostrum. After his talk the sombrero was passed. The collection amounted to $60. "I believe I'll come again," Potter concluded.

He was a Methodist, and when Southwestern University, at Georgetown, Texas, was being established by this church, Potter was delegated to raise $500 — not much money for a poker game but a great deal for "Christian education." Potter, with much effort, collected $200. Then he walked into a gambling hall — perhaps this was in San Angelo also. There he saw one of his friends and explained his purpose. "The cards are turning right for me today," the friend said. "How much have you collected?" "Two hundred dollars." "Let me have it." Potter knew there was no risk in letting this man have the money, no matter which way the card turned. The gambler bet the entire roll on one card; he won. As he handed the $400 to Parson Potter, he remarked, "The Lord is on our side all right." "Amen!" Potter echoed.

When the first volume of that wonderful storehouse of

information about range life, *The Trail Drivers of Texas,*
appeared in 1920, I read it and wrote these words across
Jack Potter's contribution: "Best in the book." During the
sixteen years that have passed since then, I have not
changed my opinion, and on many an occasion when I have
wanted to entertain an audience and give it some conception
of what a rollicky, abounding-in-life, young Texas trail
driver was like, I have read aloud Jack Potter's buoyant
pages on "Coming Up the Trail in 1882." I had a great
curiosity to know the man personally. When I read a feature article or two on him in the Dallas *News*, by Ramond
F. Adams, whose *Cowboy Lingo* has since been issued as a
book, my curiosity was whetted. Then in October of 1931 I
met him at Vernon, Texas, during a celebration memorializ-
ing Doan's Store and Doan's Crossing on Red River,
where passed millions of Texas longhorns over the old
Western Trail to Dodge City and on north clear to the
Canadian line.

He and Ab Blocker and Bob Lauderdale and I talked
away the most of one night. Just to look at him made me
realize that I had met a man — and such men are not
common — summing up in himself the whole trail driver
and range tradition. About this time Jack Potter began
contributing reminiscent articles to the *Union County
Leader,* published weekly at his home, Clayton, New
Mexico. I got him to send the paper to me, and I have
clipped every one of his articles. Some of them in slightly
changed form were reprinted in *Ranch Romances, New
Mexico Highway Magazine,* and elsewhere. In 1935 he
issued through the press of the Clayton weekly newspaper
a pamphlet entitled "Cattle Trails of the Old West." Its

only fault is that there is not more of it. Only two hundred copies were issued, and within less than ten years they will be worth $10 a copy.

It makes me joyful to know that these stray writings are to be gathered together, somewhat organized, and put into book form. I hope that old Yaqui's ebullient propensity for taking the bridle off, throwing the skillet away, and letting the panther scream will not be curbed in his book. I have decided that the most basic difference between human beings is not between borrowers and lenders, male and female, poor and rich, white and black, New Dealers and Jeffersonian Democrats, liars and truth tellers, or any other such categorical pairings; but between literalists and people with imagination. Jack Potter's imagination is a joy; his fancy, when he turns it loose, is as refreshing as a rain on a drouth-browned mesa. Anybody with any sense can tell when he's stretching the blanket; the others don't count. Here is the stuff of history, it being understood that history is something more than naked literalness.

I am assured that the original shagginess and cowpen flavor of the old Lead Steer's composition have not been edited out of it and his language made too polite. Of course every language must be translated if it is to be read by people who do not speak it. The individual qualities of the language of the range, however, lie as far beyond words peculiar to the range occupation as Shakespeare's style lies beyond the dictionary definitions of the words he uses. I quote a passage here from a letter written by that bully old range man, Teddy Blue, of the Three Deuce Ranch, Gilt Edge, Montana: "Several writers have come here and I would tell them a lot and they would write it up and quote

39

me and make me out to be a dam fool liar to all these old cowpunchers around here. The trouble is they don't talk my language and don't understand what I tell them."

In order to make absolutely sure that some of Jack Potter's original form of expression is retained in this book of his, I am going to quote extracts from a few of his letters to me. Every one of the letters is littered with enough "roadbrands" — his name for postscripts — to mark the Chisholm Trail. His principle of spelling is that of Davy Crockett's, and his typewriter is even stronger on this principle than he is. People don't intersperse their talk with "period," "comma," "capital," "new paragraph," etc. Why should people pay attention to such matters when they talk on paper? I'll admit, however, that in transferring these snatches of letters to the printed page I am putting in a few periods, etc.

When Yaqui was elected to the New Mexico state legislature in the fall of 1932, the joyful news came to me with this comment on the campaign:

I believe I have told more lies and talked more Spanish and eaten more chili than I ever did in my life before in such a short time. I may get hard to hold, but I had rather have the honor of having been a common drag driver on one of the northern cattle trails than be a dam legislator. Poetry has been written about the longhorn and the men that drove him, but who ever heard of poetry about a common legislator?

. . . I have been loosing considerable sleep thinking about some way of getting you weaned off from that brush country. The first letter I had from you, you were off down on Pena Creek looking up brands cut on rock. In the next letter you were homesick for the brasada and heading back into it. I am at a loss to know how to

40

address this. I started to address it to Nopal P. O. in care of Kerr's store, and then I commenced thinking I had not seen the name of this place in print for fifty years. I conclude that the nopals and mesquites have crowded it out of existence. Back in '79 I was with a cattle outfit wintering up the Frio River 15 miles from Nopal. We used a pack outfit to bring our supplies from that place, and the country was so brushy we had to put rawhide leggins on the packs. . . .

Sometimes a person does not have to ask questions to find out things. While running the Fort Sumner ranch I hired many cowpunchers. Some of them would start in today and quit tomorrow, and many a one after filling up on Pecos water would get the bellyache and be ready to move on. In hiring new men we always let them select a saddle rope and a stake rope. When it came to measuring off a saddle rope, a Californian would measure off about sixty feet, a prairie puncher about forty feet, and a brush popper would stop at twenty-five feet. I would ask him, "Were you ever down around Nueces town?" "You mean the Motts? Hell, yes, I was raised there."

I have been in a bushel of trouble lately. The other day an ancient looking old maid blew in from the north. She was an author and claimed she came several hundred miles to see me. She said that as the author of much wild literature I ought to be able to explain what the difference was between the east side and the west side of the Pecos. She told me that my name was too mild for the literature I was putting out. This was the first time I had ever been accused of being an author and I don't know but what she was right about my name. She told me to study up some change for it. The first thing came to my mind was Jack Yaqui Potter. She said that wouldn't do. I told her I had two fine friend authors who were pretty handy with their J's; so I suggested J. Bronco Potter or J. Burro Potter. We compromised by using my middle name, and so from now on it will be J. Myers Potter. Show this to J. Evetts Haley. I want you all to know I am the same old Jack. I believe I ought to have selected J. Burro Potter.

41

... You ask if a deer scents while asleep. My experience is limited. I have a good scent in one way. It used to be that when ever butcher killed four-year-old steers for beef, I could smell that flavor all over town while being cooked. Now when people are bound to eat young beef you can pass by a cafe shop and hardly know it.

*Dear Pancho: Pardon my delay in answering your letter. When I offer my excuse you will find I have been a very busy man. I believe I have been shadowed every day and night since my return from Vernon. The seekers after those seven burro loads of placer gold buried out east of here on the old Santa Fe Trail got the idea that I had pulled one on them when I went down there to Vernon and met you. They thought I got a lineup on their treasure. Then when a nice pasteboard box came from you containing that *Vaquero of the Brush Country* book, the word passed around that it was full of maps. They would not listen to me but wanted to take the matter up with you. I gave them your Mexico address as follows Senor Don Jotah Francisco Adobe y Byler, oficino de Senor Don Griego Sandoval y Ulibarri, Numero Dos Mil cuatro cientos y tres, Calle de Chiricahua, en frente de la Plaza de Guadalupe Hidalgo, Ciudad de Mexico, Republica de Mexico. They wanted me to write the address down. I told them they would have to take it cold from the shoulder.

They have kind of eased up during the holidays. I told them you were spending your Xmas with Death Valley Scotty, and I expect Scotty will have a big mail.

My clientage asked many questions about what kind of a superior man you were and your habits. I told them that you were a dreamer and had rather dream about longhorn cattle than gold, and that the scientist claimed you had an X-ray eye and could see clear thru a mountain. I said this was nothing

---

* Frank Dobie's publication of *Coronado's Children,* containing stories on legends and lore, buried treasures and lost mines, caused the crowd of gold seekers to follow him wherever he went. They seemed to think that Dobie had the power or knowledge of how to locate these riches. He often went under an assumed name to avoid these people.

more than what we call hawk eyed. I told them that when you made a date and came to a certain place, the people engaging you would sometimes have to wait a day or two for you to go into a trance and that they would have a high powered car setting in front of a hotel with a chauffeur in the seat and when one of these spells came on that you would rush down out of your room into the lobby and say "Vente" to whoever was waiting. I told them that in the City of Mexico you once went to that buried treasure of Montezuma's amounting to seventeen million dollars in seventeen minutes. I told them that you wanted one hundred dollars per minute for actual time in service. They asked me to engage you at that price providing you would take your pay out of the seven burro loads of placer gold already referred to as being on the old Santa Fe Trail. I told them you were that kind of fellow all right, that you didn't want something for nothing. You had better drop in one of these days and do the job. It would be a great relief to me. This is only part of what I told them.

We are having a big three day dance here commencing on Jan. 14. They got me to turn out my whiskers and contribute a wild story once a week to the home paper, the *Union County Leader*. These articles are censored by my women folks. I am sending you some of the clippings. This hombre The Bishop I talk about is no one but Jack Potter himself, a nickname I brought from the Pecos to this country. A man would be considered a weakling and not ambitious if he did not show himself up once and a while. Shopping on horseback was practiced here for several years.

After reading what you wrote in that article about telling the truth in a lying way I have studied over the matter and resolved never to tell another lie only at a regular reunion of the trail drivers and then only in a defensive way when it becomes necessary to keep up the reputation of the trail drivers.

I hope you had a fine holiday and am sending greetings. I will be more prompt next time in writing. Whenever I get about so ornery in my correspondence, I put a rope in soak and beat myself over the head with it. It generally throws fresh life into a fellow. Con salude y felicidad, Your Bueno Amigo,

JACK POTTER.

In one of his letters, Jack Potter wrote with pardonable pride, "I believe I understand all the delicate parts of the disposition of cattle." The longhorn made more history than any other breed of the taurine world, and I have a thousand times thought what a pity it is that some person of intelligence, experience, and power of observation of Jack Potter or Charles Goodnight should not have been able to assemble data in an orderly way and write a natural history book on the Texas longhorn. Time and again I have asked questions to draw old Yaqui out on the subject. The following is a letter that he wrote from Santa Fe, February 1, 1935:

> This is Sunday and as my compadres go home at the weeks end, I am what you might call a lonesome cowboy. I have been musing over the delicate parts of the dispositions of cattle and horses. I am going to tell you the truth about the native Mexican cattle before the Texas herds invaded Mexico.
> In breeding they were not near as good as the Texas longhorns. They were smaller in size and in horns. Up to the time of the closing of the Santa Fe Trail most of the steers were used as bueys [work oxen]. Goats and mutton were used more for flesh meat than steers. These native cattle never drifted far in blizzards. They were likely to stop at the first creek that had banks high enough to shelter them from the cold winds. After the storm was over a crowd of Mexicans would go south. Then when they struck a drift bunch, they would round them up closely, take down their rawhide whips, and start them off in a gallop. The cattle would make a bee line for their home range. It might be twenty or thirty miles away. The Mexican vaqueros

44

after chasing them a while, whipping them as best they could, would leave them to travel the rest of the way alone and go on to find another bunch.

In the years of 1884 and 1885 there must have been thirty or forty thousand head of Texas heifers turned loose in the Fort Sumner country. Dillard R. Fant alone delivered ten thousand head. From that time on the blizzards would drift many thousands of these cattle to the Rio Hondo or the Capitan Mountains, a hundred miles away. The longhorn drift would take the native Mexican cattle with them. The Mexican population were superstitious and claimed their cattle did not drift prior to the death of Billy the Kid and his bunch. They called one of these drifts El Partido de los Animos (The Herd of the Spirits) and claimed that the spirits of Billy the Kid and his followers O'Folliard and Bowdre were causing the trouble.

Once after we had been working several weeks coming up the Pecos, we finished rounding up at the Bosque Redondo just above Fort Sumner. We had in the herd a two year old Mexican heifer branded with a small Mexican stamp letter. We called any animal of this Mexican breed a Bueno.* Working in the outfit was a good old hard-working cowboy who had just started himself a brand, the N. T., with the N over the T. I said to him, "John, nobody knows anything about that heifer's ownership. The brand on her is too little to count anyway. You just run her off to one side and run your N T on her." Sure enough he did this. When he let her up she was on the peck good and proper. She ran into his horse. Then she headed off south through the sandhills, moving like she was going somewhere.

About ten days later this old cowboy was sent as outside man to join the roundups in the Capitan Mountains, a hundred miles to the south. In those days everyone tried to advertise his brand, and John had that N T brand of his carved into his leather hat band, on his leather cuffs, on his spur leathers, on

---

* Bueno: An unclaimed animal with unrecorded brand supposed to have passed inspection by trail cutters and inspectors (see *Cowboy Lingo* by Raymond F. Adams).

the leather band around his bed roll, and everywhere else he could find room to put it.

Well, at the very first roundup, which was at Los Tanos, a Mexican settlement, the first thing that showed up was that heifer John had branded at Bosque Redondo. An old Mexican rode out and pointing to the N T on the heifer, asked the roundup boss, *"Quien es este hierro?"* ("Whose brand is that?") You could have roped that old cowboy's eyes, they were bugged out so far when he saw the heifer. To get out of the predicament he galloped off to camp and commenced defacing the N T from his bed roll strop, hat band, etc.

The only thing I hate about Santa Fe is the inscription on that monument in the plaza. You no doubt have read it. (It is hard on the Confederacy.) When I raise my head, the Sangre de Cristo snow-capped range looms up with her hidden secrets of four hundred years of tragedies, feasts and famines. It is interesting to ride out on the outskirts of Santa Fe and see those large crosses on the tops of most of the hills where the natives used to take those Spanish priests and shoot them.

Well, be as good as you ought to be. According to the George Saunders *Grammar,* you can tell a whole lot if you give him time and space.

Your old Compadre.

I come back to the gush of humanity that wells up in Jack Potter, the warmth of hearty animal spirits, the positive genius for conviviality that is his. To be free with him is far more inspiring than drink, but we have indulged a world of foolery over the subject of liquor. His lust for good fellowship and his generosity of spirits is better than a mountain breeze. Once Evetts Haley got hold of a quart of corn whiskey distilled by an old German down in Washington County, Texas, and took it to Jack Potter. This is one of several allusions to it: "I will expect you and

46

J. Evetts some time after getting a consignment of that Washington County remedio to work up a little inspiration and write me a joint letter."

Nobody else has ever so made me go the whole length in foolery — get drunk on it. But I am trying to bell the old Lead Steer himself and not lead myself out. I wanted to quote a letter I wrote, but Jack Potter says he wore it out showing it around. I wanted to show how the old Lead Steer makes the bell go clapper. I think his reminiscences will do that anyhow.

Austin, Texas

A Salute to
Gene Rhodes

"CAN YOU TELL ME why the work of Eugene Manlove Rhodes is not better known?" asked a contributor to the second issue of the *Saturday Review of Literature*, August 2, 1924.

As to literature, this man's writings have a variety of charms; in sensitive, vivid description; in clear characterizations; in an easy, light-running style, warm with humor and brilliant with wit. In time, place, and character, he is American of the Americans. His stories are fresh and original. He is himself a reader; his work is continuously pricked and sparkling with allusion and lightly touched quotation, filling the mind with a sense of old friendships close at hand. There ought to be a good library edition of the works of Mr. Rhodes.

The writer of this appraisal belonged to the "passionate few" who, according to Arnold Bennett, make and maintain the fame of classical authors. The critical passion of the few that keeps many classics alive resulted, in 1946, in the private publication of a collection of stray stories and verses by Eugene Manlove Rhodes under the title of *The Little World Waddies*.

The readers of it were not confined to the "passionate

few" any more than were the readers of Rhodes's novels serialized for years in the *Saturday Evening Post* and then of the same novels in book form. On the author known familiarly as Gene Rhodes, I ask for no better judges than the waddies themselves — the ones who read. During World War II, Captain Tom Hickman, who used to ride as cowboy and Texas ranger, came to see me. We talked about R. B. Cunninghame Graham — who wrote so well of South American gauchos and Spanish horses — and about Gene Rhodes.

Back in 1924, while Tom Hickman was on his way to England with Tex Austin's rodeo, he stayed in New York a few days and went up to Apalachin to call on his favorite writer of the West. There May Rhodes told him something only lightly intimated in her very human book about her husband. She said that a passion for playing poker kept Gene poor even while he was selling stories at a good rate. Gene "didn't care for money." May Rhodes showed the cowboy from Texas a file of correspondence between Gene and some individual in New York who also liked to play poker. The five letters read as follows:

"Come down."

"Can't come."

"Why?"

"Broke."

"Sad."

Eugene Manlove Rhodes put Cole Railston into more than one of his stories. Cole Railston was range foreman for the Bar N Cross when, about 1889, Gene came to work for it. Cole was a very young boss then; now he lives on his own modest ranch out from Magdalena, New Mexico, and reads and remembers and reflects. Perhaps no other man so combines knowledge of Gene Rhodes's life as a cowboy with appreciation of him as a writer.

"Gene grew and spread after leaving our Bar Cross outfit at Engle," Cole Railston wrote me in a letter.

He was a remarkable character. About 1905 he put out a little story called "The Last Guard." I liked it best of all his writings. Should you know of any way to find it, I wish you would get one or a dozen copies for me.

As to the kind of cowboy he made, while Gene worked for me on summer roundups some three seasons, his job was mostly to care for the saddle horses, but the last summer he was a cowhand. Gene never claimed to be a top hand, but he was an all-around good hand. On day herd, night guard, or in the branding-pen, he was loyal, tireless, and fearless. There is no question about Gene's courage in the wild work of duty and danger. They used to say jokingly that young Rhodes carried a book instead of a gun. I never knew him to carry a pistol. I believe he liked to herd the saddle horses because that work gave him more time for reading. The boys all liked him. Next to cowboying and reading, he liked poker and a fight. He was not a troublemaker, far from it, but no one stepped on his toes or rode his pet horse. I never knew any man to throw Gene in a wrestling match. He feared no bad man or bad horse. He was a real good rough bronc rider. Send him anywhere to be gone from the roundup wagon for a day or so, and he made no fuss about bed or food. He simply went, did the job, and came back smiling.

The first novel of any consequence to be published about the range, *The Virginian,* in 1902, is deft on situations and the code of men of spurs, but Owen Wister was not looking at range life from the inside. His cowboys do not work with cows. In *The Log of a Cowboy,* by Andy Adams, published in 1903, the men — and no women belong here

— are never away from cows and horses. If all literature on whales and whalers were destroyed with the exception of *Moby Dick,* we could still get from that novel a just conception of the occupation of whaling. If, excepting *The Log of a Cowboy,* all literature pertaining to trail herds, to the seas of unfenced grass and to the sinewy men who "rattled their hocks" behind longhorn cattle from the Rio Grande to the Plains of Alberta were destroyed, we could still get from the homemade classic that Andy Adams wrote a just conception of range-riding and trail-driving.

The riders that ride so free through Rhodes's fiction are usually separated from their cows, but they are infused by the fact — including the code — of their occupation. Their eyes are used to looking through heat devils shimmering over drouth-browned mesas and at mountains a look and a half away. Without their knowing it, something of the tonic of sagebrush aroma has passed into the very corpuscles of their blood and something of the assurance belonging to the quietness of sky and earth has entered into their mental attitudes. They cannot be called earthy characters; the created components of their nature are sometimes too apparent; but they always belong to the Land of Little Rain.

Aside from their inherent decency, their most distinguishing characteristic is the vivacity of their talk. It is never glib; it is often witty; it is uniformly natural. The culmination of the art of writing as Eugene Manlove Rhodes practiced it, so it seems to me, is in this talk. It constantly fulfills Stevenson's direction — Stevenson, who in Rhodes's opinion "used the English tongue more skillfully than any other man" — to have characters talk "not

as men talk in parlors, but as they might talk." This talk
may be homely and earthy. "We'll wash our hands and
faces right good, catch us up some fresh horses out of the
pasture, and terrapin up the road a stretch." It may be, and
often is, as lightsome as the white smoke from mesquite
coals in a serene campfire; it may occasionally be dark with
human destiny; it repeatedly glints and gleams with literary
allusions. Yet no bright speaker ever sacrifices fidelity to
his own naturalness or to the flavor of the earth to which
he belongs in order to say a good thing.

"You give me that un," thundered Marshal Yewell, of
The Trusty Knaves.

Pres Lewis took a square of plug tobacco from his pocket, scruti-
nized it, selected a corner, and gnawed a segment from it. "You
keep your voice down, brother," he said, restoring the mutilated plug
to its pocket. "If you bellow at me any more, I'm liable to prophesy
against you. You just turn your mind back and see what happened
when people crowded me into foretelling. When you got any com-
munications for me, I wan 'em sweet and low, like the wind of the
western sea."

The girl in *Bransford of Rainbow Range* considered,
"What manner of cowboy was this, from whose tongue a
learned scientific term tripped spontaneously in so stressful
a moment — who quoted scraps of The Litany unaware?"
It is the Eugene Manlove Rhodes "manner of cowboy."
And the manner belonged to the Rhodes who night-herded
and day-herded, too, as well as to the Rhodes who wove
out of experience and imagination those gay riders named
John Wesley Pringle, Johnny Dines, Jeff Bransford, Ross
McEwen, Ptomaine Tommy, and a cavalcade of others.

Their individualism goes deeper than bowlegs and the you-all drawl. They can all read, write, and recollect. They have read; they combine in themselves generosity with that you-be-damned air; they are utterly at ease on the planet that their author "recommended" as being "a good place to spend a lifetime"; they carry "bottles of salvation" filled with uncorked champagne-natured mother wit.

"Thanks, but you are a teetotaler?" said Jeff Bransford.

"A — well — not exactly," stammered Aughinbaugh. "But I have to be very careful. I — I only take one drink at a time!" He fumbled out another glass.

"I stumble, I stumble!" said Bransford gravely. He poured out a small drink and passed the bottle. "I fill this cup to one made up!" He held the glass up to the light.

"Well?" said Aughinbaugh expectantly. "Go on!"

"That description can't be bettered," said Bransford.

Now it's John Wesley Pringle speaking. "You had all the material to build a nice plump hunch. It all went over your head. You put me in mind of the lightning bug.

> The lightning bug is brilliant,
> But it hasn't any mind;
> It wanders through creation
> With its headlight on behind."

The Bernheimer Oriental Gardens at Pacific Palisades, California, no longer exist, but what was their chief adornment will always exist for me. There among the flowers, a bronze figure of a Chinese philosopher sits at ease on a water buffalo, absorbed in a book, while the understanding beast carries him to whatever may be his destination. It is an exquisite piece of work, both joyful and placid. I want to contribute to a fund for erecting a bronze figure of Eugene Manlove Rhodes, at whatever may be the most appropriate spot in New Mexico. I want the figure to be of Gene reading a book on a gentle cow horse manifestly in harmony with the philosophy of his rider. As horse wrangler he used to snake up wood for the camp cook. He would rope some poles, wrap the rope around the horn of his saddle, head his horse for camp, take out one of the books he habitually carried in saddle pocket or coat pocket, and lose himself in the pages as the horse walked along. A woman on a lone, lone ranch in New Mexico told me how she looked out the window one day and saw Gene Rhodes reading a book on his horse, which had stopped at the yard gate. She saw that he was oblivious to everything but the imagined world and went on about her work until, about half an hour later, seeing that Gene had not moved except to turn the page, she called to him to get down and come in. "I guess I will," he replied. "That's what I rode over here for."

He once complained that the ranch people seemed to be remembering him more for reading than for riding. In his cowboy days he gloried in hanging with the highest pitchers and the crookedest twisters, but his idea of a "broke" horse was one broken to the sound of paper-rustling as well as to the saddle. One bronc he rode would rear over backward upon hearing a page turned; Gene always stepped clear, holding to the bridle reins. Once, after stepping clear, he grabbed the horse's head while the horse was still down and sat on it reading a volume of Browning's poetry until, presumably, the bronc had absorbed something of literary usage.

The memorable time I visited Cole Railston on his ranch, I asked him if Gene Rhodes had a model for the extraordinary facility with which certain cowboys in his fiction make literary allusions, generally obliquely, and quote verse, both doggerel and classic.

"It might have been Bill Barbee," Cole Railston answered, and then, in his rich way, he went ahead to sketch Bill Barbee.

When Bill Barbee rode into Marfa that time to catch a westbound train, he and his ga'nted horse both looked suspicious to some Texas rangers stationed there. They arrested him, searched him, questioned him. They consulted their book of "wanted men." Then they reported to Captain Hughes that, although they felt certain this stranger was "wanted," they could not find a single identifying clue.

"Anything in his vest pocket?" the captain asked.

"Yes, a little notebook with some pages torn out and not a name, date, or place in it."

"Let's see the notebook."

The prisoner was present and he handed out his notebook. The captain opened it. On the inside of the front cover he saw a B with a horizontal line — a bar — under it, and, under the bar, another B. Cowboys have brands even if they own nothing but spur-leathers to put the brand on. A favorite form of brand is a rebus. The captain looked at the B combined with bar and B. He looked at the prisoner.

"Bill Bar-bee," he said.

"I always heard you were a dictionary on brands," Bill Barbee answered.

The rangers had him on their list. He was wanted for what he considered a killing of honor — not a murder. He had ordered his sister not to marry a certain man; she persisted; he made the man unmarriageable. Not long after the arrest a jury decided that Bill Barbee's interpretation of honor was too liberal and detained him at Huntsville two years before he went to work for the Bar Cross in New Mexico, under Cole Railston. Gene Rhodes was working for the outfit at the time. He told Cole Railston how he first met Barbee.

Along late one evening, alone in camp and standing beside his cabin, he saw a strange cowboy riding up. The stranger fulfilled all of Gene's dreams of the gallant cowboy-ee. He was dressed cap-a-pie just right, not a mite overdressed, the crease in his Stetson both distinguished and careless. He rode as "active-valiant" as Hotspur. After he had dismounted, he walked with a walk marked but not marred by times in the saddle. He was as alert as his spur jinglè; he had the reserve that belongs to nature's modesty. Inside the cabin his eye fell on the table of books that his host kept, a volume of Shakespeare dominant among them.

"Now there's something about that second soliloquy in *Richard the Third*," Bill Barbee said.

But Gene Rhodes had been putting this ideal cowboy into another kind of story. Right at this point, he wanted to get a bit of horse lore from him. Three times he shifted the subject, and each time the visitor came back to *Richard the Third.* He quoted all of the soliloquy. He could quote Shakespeare like Leviticus quoting the Good Book itself.

I have spruced Bill Barbee up. Yet he may well have served for one model. "I cribbed that remark from Billy Beebe," says John Wesley Also-Ran Pringle in *The Desire of the Moth.* Rhodes often transmuted real people into book characters. If a writer does not steal, he naturally has to borrow. John Wesley Pringle would have talked in his way, however, had Bill Barbee never existed. He came out of Gene Rhodes himself. "I have a woodshed where I can retire to split an infinitive with a friend," he wrote. He proposed to an editor a column for letter-writers, "where the liar and the lamb can lie down together."

He seems to have felt under compulsion to justify his literary-allusioning cowboys. "They all smoked," he explains in *Bransford of Rainbow Range* — smoked Bull Durham tobacco.

A certain soulless corporation placed in each package of the tobacco a coupon, each coupon redeemable by one paper-bound book. . . . There were three hundred and three volumes on that list, mostly — but not altogether — fiction. And each one was a classic. Classics are cheap. They are not copyrighted. . . . Cowboys all smoked, and the most deep-seated instinct of the human race is to get something for nothing. They got those books. In due course of time they read those books. Some were slow to take to it; but when you stay at lonely ranches, when you are left afoot until the waterholes dry up, so you may catch a horse in the waterpen — why, you must do something. The books were read. Then, having acquired the habit, they bought more books. Since the three hundred and three were all real books, and since the cowboys had been previously uncorrupted of predigested or sterilized fiction, or by "gift," "uplift," and "helpful" books, their composite taste had become surprisingly good, and they bought with discriminating care.

This account of literary pursuits in the cow camps varies slightly from that given by Gene Rhodes's admired friend Charlie Siringo, in the Preface to *A Texas Cowboy, or Fifteen Years on the Hurricane Deck of a Spanish Pony*. In this first-published of all cowboy autobiographies, rollicky Charlie Siringo recollected:

While ranching on the Indian Territory line, close to Caldwell, Kansas, in the winter of '82 and '83, we boys — there being nine of us — made an ironclad rule that whoever was heard swearing or caught picking grey backs off and throwing them on the floor without first killing them, should pay a fine of ten cents for each and every offense. The proceeds to be used for buying choice literature — something that would have a tendency to raise us above the average cowpuncher. Just twenty-four hours after making this rule we had three dollars in the pot — or at least in my pocket, I having been appointed treasurer.

As I was going to town that night to see my Sunday girl, I proposed to the boys that, while up there, I send the money off for a year's subscription to some good newspaper. The question came up, what paper shall it be? We finally agreed to leave it to a vote — each man to write the one of his choice on a slip of paper and drop it in a hat. There being two young Texans present who could neither read nor write, we let them speak their choice after the rest of us got our votes deposited. At the word given them to cut loose they both yelled *"Police Gazette,"* and on asking why they voted for that wicked sheet, they both replied as though with one voice, "Cause we can read the pictures." We found, on counting the votes, that the *Police Gazette* had won, so it was subscribed for.

But Charlie Siringo's cowboys were from southern Texas, where to this day many of their descendants suspect literature that rises to the plane of having ideas as being "subversive," and, therefore, as not to be trusted; also, where boiled frijoles have for generations been much more common than canned goods. New Mexico cowboys, even those "who could not read at all," became letter-perfect in finishing off "any sudden quotation from the labels of such cans, bags, sacks or other containers as were used for standard brands of coffee, sugar, flour, condensed milk, pears, peaches and other such." Rhodes might have added to what he thus wrote, in *Beyond the Desert,* that it never was settled whether "ozs." was to be recited as "ozzes" or "ounces." Anyway, the exercise is supposed to have induced excellence of memories in quoting literature.

Despite the pretenses of advertisements of the classics and despite the practices of book review clubs, nobody ever read seriously for the purpose of displaying familiarity with literature; least of all, Eugene Manlove Rhodes. In *Say Now Shibboleth,* he rejects the idea that a writer should read the great writers "for style." He says,

Read the great dead masters for ideas. Devour them, Fletcherize them, digest, assimilate, make them part of your blood; let the enriched blood visit your brain. The resultant activities will be fairly your own, and the little kinks and convolutions of your brain, which are entirely different from the kinks of any other brain, will furnish you all the style you will ever get.

A newspaper article about Eugene Manlove Rhodes by a very thoughtful historian of the West characterizes him as "a bold, gallant, card-playing, pool-playing, cowpunching natural son of the American West." It is this Philistine conception of what constitutes natural sons that makes the civilized pursuit of art and ideas so difficult everywhere in America and especially in the Southwest. The passionate few are not passionate in their regard for Eugene Manlove Rhodes because he was a card-playing cowpuncher; they are passionate toward him because of the way his cultivated mind played upon the cowpuncher world. One part of him was a part of this world, but the "immortal residue" of him was beyond it — the part that justified Bernard De Voto in calling his fiction the only fiction of the cattle country "that reaches a level which it is intelligent to call art." Being a good hand on horseback did not make Gene Rhodes a good writer, though pride and vitality are common denominators of both.

True art always transcends the provincial. Gene Rhodes loved his waddie land and its people passionately. He made that land more interesting, gave it significance, added something of the spirit to its expanses. We dwellers upon it must feel an abiding gratitude to him. His art, however, is to be judged not by what he translated into books, but by how he translated it. He died before the basic fact — along with oceans of jargon — of our One World had sunk into the minds of the thinking minority of this country; but the assimilation of ideas from the earth's great thinkers and writers had made him conscious of the harmony between loyalty to one province and indebtedness to provinces beyond. In *The Proud Sheriff*, Andy Hinkle reports to Spinal Maginnis on the people "hither," whence he has just returned. "Fine people. Just like here. Nine decent men for every skunk. Nine that hate treachery and lies and hoggishness and dirt. They got different ways."

"But you think our ways are best?"

"I would never say so. I think our ways are different."

The people foreign to Rhodes were what he called "The Tumblebug People." He was sensitive to injustice anywhere. He wrote "In Defense of Pat Garrett," who had been maligned by Walter Noble Burns in a jingoistic attempt to Robin Hood that cold-blooded murderer and horse thief known as Billy the Kid. He would not linger in Socorro because he "had seen a man stamped to death in front of the post office." He wanted to organize the whole West into resenting aspersions on its manhood and womanhood by Stuart Henry — aspersions hardly worth noticing. He never attained to the amplitude of Mark Twain, but inside his own confining range he was blood brother to that genius who wrote books out of righteous wrath to defend Joan of Arc and Harriet Shelley and to expose hypocrisies in religion. More than two hundred years after Don Diego Dionisio de Peñalosa had ridden in the land of the Apache and espoused the cause of the "copper-colored children of the New World" against their Christianizing enslavers and, for reward, been indicted as *embustero* (liar) by the Spanish Inquisition, Eugene Manlove Rhodes flamed to salute him as "first in America to strike a blow for freedom, first to dare the Inquisition."

He stood for "the little people" against important
oppressors.
Lo, we have dreamed down slavery, and we have
dreamed down kings,
And still we dream of decency and the end of evil
things.

A Mexican sheepherder is saved from being lynched by greed, and a poor squatter from being ousted by more greed. The savior, in Rhodes's stories, is always witty as well as decent, debonair as well as just. The hero's being a cowboy is secondary to his believing in something. Rhodes was not a sociological righter of a system's wrongs in the manner of Upton Sinclair. He did not understand systems, and being a man of intellectual integrity, he did not pretend to understand them. He more or less accepted them — as systems. He stood on the principle of applied democracy. For him, "a man's a man for a' that" was poetry only incidentally; primarily it was eternal verity. His nearest kinsman was Cyrano de Bergerac — with whom he would have uncovered to "that divine madman," Don Quixote.

And what should a man do? Attain to height by craft instead of by strength? No, I thank you. Push himself from lap to lap, become a little great man in a great little circle? No, I thank you. But . . . sing, dream, laugh, loaf, be free, have eyes that look squarely, a voice with a ring; wear, if he chooses, his hat hindside afore; for a yes, for a no, fight a duel or turn a ditty! Work, without concern of fortune or of glory, to accomplish the heart's desired journey to the moon! Put forth nothing that has not its spring in the very heart, yet, modest, say to himself, "Old man, be satisfied with blossoms, fruits, yea, leaves alone, so they be gathered in your garden and no other man's!"

It was righteous indignation against an ignorant definition of the cowboy as "never anything more than a hired hand on horseback" that produced — despite a dead tree's "lashing fate" — not only the finest poem yet written on any range subject but the strongest, noblest and most moving poem that the Southwest can claim.

> Merry eyes and tender eyes, dark head and bright . . .
> Doggerel upon his lips and valor in his heart . . .
> The hired man on horseback goes laughing to his
> work . . .
> The hired man on horseback has raised the rebel yell.

"No better description of Gene's romantic years will ever be written" than these lines give, May Rhodes well says. He was about to be sixty when he wrote them. His best years were the romantic years; he was still amid the romantic years when he died. His best characters are constitutionally generous, gay, and gallant because he himself was constitutionally generous, gay, and gallant. I do not mean gallant in the self-esteeming *caballero* sense, but gallant in prodigal selflessness, in upholding a principle, in being ready to charge hell with a bucket of water, to take the side of the wronged, "to find quarrel in a straw when honour's at the stake." As he has Jeff Bransford put it, "Speaking the truth comes easier for them than for some folks, 'cause if speaking the aforesaid truth displeases anyone, they mostly don't give a damn."

Whoever wants the full and flavored facts about the life of Gene Rhodes will find them in *The Hired Man on Horseback* by May Rhodes. He was born in Nebraska, January 19, 1869, to a family of homesteaders. Prairie fires, grasshoppers, and cyclones drove them to Kansas, where they homesteaded and suffered plagues again. Then in 1881 they came to New Mexico and filed on another homestead. There were always some good books for the children to read and scanty schooling. When he was thirteen, riding a saddle bought with soap coupons, Gene got a job with a cow outfit. For seven years he drew cowboy wages. Then he borrowed fifty dollars from his father and for two years, living mainly on oatmeal, attended a college at San Jose, California. Here a wider choice of literature fertilized him and he practiced writing.

Now he was back in the saddle, though he taught a country school for a spell. He had a little ranch of his own in the San Andres Mountains. He was better at riding horses and driving cows than he was at ownership; he valued other things higher than he valued property. A young widow named May Davison Purple in a faraway village called Apalachin, in the state of New York, read one of his poems and wrote him of her appreciation. He was thirty when, riding a cattle train, he followed his letters to her home and married her. After three years of ranch life, Mrs. Rhodes went back to Apalachin; Gene soon followed and stayed for twenty years, developing as a story writer, also as a poker player. In 1926 the two returned with their son Alan to New Mexico, lingered a few years, and then moved to California, where, still writing, Gene died, June 27, 1934.

Toward sundown one September day in 1940, I headed west out of Tularosa, New Mexico, with the intention of camping at the water beside which Gene Rhodes used to live. I was alone and had my camping outfit in the car. During the twenty-five-mile drive across the sands and alkali flats I did not meet or see a soul. It was way after dark when I got among the boulders of Rhodes Canyon. I stopped to eat a supper of bread, cheese, and an apple. Soon after I got out of the car I saw headlights coming the way I had come. I had finished eating and, standing against my car door, was filling my pipe when the oncomer halted beside me.

"Having trouble?" a hearty voice asked.

"No, I thank you."

"What part of Texas you from?"

"Austin."

"Let's drink to Old Texas." The stranger was already dangling a pint bottle out the car window.

"I've come to this canyon to spend the night on the ground where Gene Rhodes used to rattle his spurs," I said. "Let's drink to his cheerful soul."

"I helped bury him. Here's to Gene. Follow me and I'll show you where to spread your bedroll."

We rode on a good while. My guide knew the gullies, boulders, and sharp curves and was more strongly fortified against all tame considerations of security than I was. Finally I caught up with him where he had halted. "Gene's cabin used to be over there," he said. "You can drive down close to the water and have a level place to camp on."

I never slept a more freeing sleep. I washed in the cool, fresh water, boiled coffee in it, and filled a jug. I gathered some wild verbena next to Gene's old corral. "Gene was considered wild," they say — wild like the free flowers. I felt freer and gladder and richer because he had lived and said what he said. May Rhodes tells me that she still has the pressed wild flowers.

On up the slope, I stopped in the New Mexico sunshine and walked to the grave. It is where Gene Rhodes wanted it, alone in the San Andres Mountains, overlooking the pass that bears his name. A bronze plaque on a great boulder bears the epitaph of supreme fitness.

"PASO POR AQUI"
EUGENE MANLOVE RHODES
January 19, 1869–June 27, 1934

Had he written nothing else but *Pasó por Aquí,* the passion of the few would persist. My copy of this story, bound with *Once in the Saddle,* is inscribed with black ink, and on the pages that follow, Monte's Spanished-English is corrected with red lead. What artist with words — in a phrase from Eddy Orcutt's fine essay on Rhodes — conscious of "the salt and glory of our language," ever escaped the gross luminosity given by print to his own imperfections? There is nothing to change in the story's finality on human dignity, decency, and gallantry. On the flyleaf of my copy of *Pasó por Aquí* Gene Rhodes wrote, "Why is joy not considered a fit subject for an artist?" He never wrote the last book he wanted to write. He did write the concluding sentence for it — a farewell salute to the "gay, kind, and fearless." That salute is for you, also, one of the "Masterless Men," you Eugene Cyrano de Bergerac Manlove Rhodes!

The Conservatism of
Charles M. Russell

ONE CANNOT IMAGINE Charles M. Russell living in a
world without horses. If the wheel had never been devised,
he could have lived content. The steamboat had carried
traders and trappers up the Missouri River and become a
feature in the pageant of the West before he was born; he
accepted the steamboat, respected it. When in 1880, at the
age of sixteen, he went to Montana, he traveled by the
railway to its end and then took the stage. The Far West
was at that time still an unfenced and comparatively un-
occupied expanse of grass and mountains; he accepted and
respected the steam engine as one of its features. As it
hauled in plows, barbed wire and people, people, people,
he would, had he had the power, have Joshuaed the sun to
a permanent standstill.

The Russell genius was averse to change. No single collection of his great art could be regarded as a full document on the evolution of transportation in the West; although in his fertile life span he came close to this. Such a
series would include the old Red River cart drawn with
such casual care in his *Pen Sketches* (about 1899). Other
able drawings and paintings, except that of the Pony
Express, focus upon conveyances, progressing from dog

travois to railroad train, that stress incident and effect upon human beings rather than the transports themselves.

Including the transports, Russell did document the Old West. Plains Indian or frontiersman dominates countless paintings. Russell never generalized. In any Russell picture of horses, for example, a particular horse at a particular time responds in a particular way to a particular stimulus; in the same way, his man-made objects are viewed under particular circumstances. Here the steamboat and railway train are interesting through the eyes of the Indians whom they are dooming, very much as in one of Russell's paintings a wagon, unseen, is interesting for the alarm that sight of its tracks over prairie grass gives a band of scouting warriors. He was positively not interested in anything bearing mechanical evolution.

C. M. Russell's passionate sympathy for the primitive West welled into antipathy for the forces relegating it — and for him automobiles and tractors expressed those forces. He never glimpsed, much less accepted, "the one increasing purpose" in evolutionary processes that enables the contemporary Texas artist, Tom Lea for example, to comprehend with equanimity and equal sympathy the conquistador riding the first horse upon an isolated continent and the airplane that, more than four hundred years afterwards, bridges continents. Each a distinct man and a distinct artist, Tom Lea is at home in a cosmopolitan world of change, whereas Charlie Russell was at home only in a West that had ceased to exist by the time he arrived at artistic maturity. Tom Lea grapples intellectually with his world, is a thinker; Charlie Russell evaluated life out of instinctive predilections. Vitality, that "one thing needful" to all creative work, shows constantly in the work of both.

Russell's opposition to change was but the obverse of his concentration upon the old. His art can be comprehended only through an understanding of his conservatism. It was not the conservatism of the privileged who resent change because change will take away their privileges. It was the conservatism of love and loyalty.

Before he died in 1926, the airplane was changing the world; he dismissed it as a "flying machine." He was fond of skunks, a family of which he protected at his lodge on Lake McDonald, but his name for the automobile was "skunk wagon." His satisfaction in a cartoon he made showing mounted Indians passing a broken-down skunk wagon is manifest. His forward-looking wife Nancy — to whom Russell's career as a serious artist was largely owing — would say to him, "Charlie, why don't you take an interest in something besides the past?" "She lives for tomorrow and I live for yesterday," he said. For a long time he refused to ride in an automobile; he never did put a hand on a steering wheel. "You can have a car," he often said to Nancy, "but I'll stick to my hoss; we understan' each other better." At the World's Fair, in 1903, at St. Louis, the place of his birth and boyhood, he passed by the exhibitions of twentieth-century progress and found kinship with a caged coyote "who licked my hand like he knew me. I guess I brought the smell of plains with me."

"Invention," he wrote to a friend, "has made it easy for mankind but it has made him no better. Machinery has no branes." He resented the advent of the electric lights as deeply, but not so quietly, as Queen Victoria. He once

called the automatic rifle a "God-damned diarrhoea gun"
— and I wonder how he would have spelled it. The old-
time six-shooter and Winchester rifle were good enough
for him. In the physical world he was a fundamentalist. It
began going to hell for him about 1889, the year that
Montana Territory became a state with ambitions to develop. One time Nancy got him to make a speech at a kind
of booster gathering. The toastmaster introduced him as a
pioneer.

Charlie began: "I have been called a pioneer. In my
book a pioneer is a man who comes to a virgin country,
traps off all the fur, kills off all the wild meat, cuts down
all the trees, grazes off all the grass, plows the roots up,
and strings ten million miles of bob wire. A pioneer de-
stroys things and calls it civilization. I wish to God that
this country was just like it was when I first saw it and
that none of you folks were here at all."

About this time he realized that he had insulted his
audience. He grabbed his hat and, in the boots and des-
perado sash that he always wore, left the room.

A string of verses that he wrote to Robert Vaughn
concludes:

> Here's to hell with the booster,
> The land is no longer free,
> The worst old timer I ever knew
> Looks dam good to me.

Russell's devotion to old times, old ways, the Old West
did not come from age. It was congenital. Even in infancy
he pictured the West of Indians, spaces and outlanders and

knew that he wanted it. Only when he got there did he begin to live. When he was forty-three years old, he looked at the "sayling car lines" (elevated) of New York and set down as a principle of life that the "two miles of railroad track and a fiew hacks" back in Great Falls were "swift enouf" for him. From Chicago in 1916 he wrote his friend and neighbor A. J. Trigg:

It's about thirty-two years since I first saw this burg. I was armed with a punch pole, a stock car under me loaded with grass eaters. I came from the big out doores and the light, smoke and smell made me lonsum. The hole world has changed since then I have not. I'm no more at home in a big city than I was then an I'm still lonsum.

He wanted room; he wanted to be left alone; he believed in other people being left alone. His last request was that his body be carried to the grave behind horses and not by a machine, and that is the way it was carried.

In one respect Charlie Russell was far ahead of his contemporaries, who generally said that the only good Indian was a dead Indian. He had profound sympathy for the Plains Indians. His indignation against sharks greedy for their land was acid. "The land hog is the only animal known that lives without a heart." He hated prohibition laws and all kinds of prohibitors; he hated fervidly white men who debauched Indians with liquor. He painted the women and children as well as warriors of several tribes, always with accuracy in physical detail and recognition of their inherent dignity. "Those Indians have been living in heaven for a thousand years," he said to cowman Teddy Blue [Granville Stuart's son-in-law], "and we took it way from 'em for forty dollars a month." When sometimes he

71

spoke of "my people" he meant the Horseback Indians. He called the white man "Nature's enemy." The Indians harmonized with Nature and had no more desire to "conquer" it or alter any aspect of it than a cottontail rabbit.

Over and over, he pictured schooners, freight wagons, packhorses, Indian buffalo hunters, cowboys, Northwest Mounted Police, horse thieves, cow thieves, stage robbers and other horseback men. Bull-whackers, mule skinners, stage drivers and their contemporaries of the frontier were as congenial to him as "Nature's cattle" — among which the coyote and the tortoise were in as good standing as the elk and the antelope and in better standing than a "cococola soke." "He can tell what's the matter with a ford by the nois it makes but he wouldn't know that a wet cold horse with a hump in his back is dangerous."

The "increasing purpose" of man's development of passenger vehicles has been to achieve more speed. Charlie Russell has often been styled the artist of Wild West action. It is true that his range bulls lock horns and his longhorn cows get on the prod, that his cowboys often shoot, that his cow horses are apt to break in two, that his grizzly bears are hungrier for hot blood than Liver-Eating Johnson; in short, that violence was with him a favorite theme. At the same time, no other picturer of the Old West has so lingered in repose. He likes cow horses resting their hips at hitching racks or standing with bridle reins "tied to the ground"; his masterpiece of range life is a trail boss sitting sideways on his horse watching a long herd stringing up a draw as slowly as "the lowing herd" of milk cows winds "o'er the lea" in Gray's *Elegy*. One of his most dramatic paintings is of shadows. The best thing in his superb story of a stampede, "Longrope's Last Guard," in *Trails Plowed Under,* is the final picture of Longrope wrapped in his blankets and put to bed on the lone prairie. "It sounds lonesome, but he ain't alone, cause these old prairies has cradled many of his kind in their long sleep."

In only some of the great paintings in the large C. M. Russell collection at the Historical Society of Montana, in Helena, does drama reside in fast or violent action. There is drama in all Russell art, but it is the drama of potentiality, of shadowing destiny, of something coming, of something left behind. Russell illustrated a little-known pamphlet entitled *Back Trailing on the Old Frontiers.* He was a great traveler in that direction; he was as cold as a frosted crowbar towards the fever for being merely, no matter how rapidly, transported, as afflicts so many Americans today.

If the Old West was important to itself, Charlie Russell was important also, for he was — in art — its most representative figure.

If the Old West is still important in any way to the modern West, Russell remains equally important. If the Old West is important to faraway lands and peoples, Charles M. Russell is important. He not only knew this West, he felt it. It moved him, motivated him, and gave him articulation, as a strong wind on some barren crag shapes all the trees that try to grow there.

Sometimes Russell lacked perspective on the whole of life. Sometimes he overdid violence and action, particularly that brand demanded by appreciators of calendars. But he never betrayed the West.

When one knows and loves the thousands of little truthful details that Charlie Russell put into the ears of horses, the rumps of antelopes, the nostrils of deer, the eyes of buffaloes, the lifted heads of cattle, the lope of coyotes, the stance of a stage driver, the watching of a shadow of himself by a cowboy, the response of an Indian storyteller, the way of a she-bear with her cub, the you-be-damned independence of a monster grizzly, the ignorance of an ambling terrapin, the lay of grass under a breeze, and a whole catalogue of other speaking details dear to any lover of Western life, then one cherishes all of Charles M. Russell.

Charlie Siringo,
Writer and Man

CHARLES A. SIRINGO was born in Matagorda County,
Texas, February 7, 1855, and he died in Hollywood, California, October 19, 1928. Angelo Siringo, the census report of 1860 has the name; he was known to thousands
simply as Charlie Siringo. For the first eleven years of his
life he was his "folks' contrary son." For the next fifteen
years or so he was a cowboy; then, for two decades, a
detective. Thereafter his life, lived mostly in New Mexico
and California, was meager and splattered, some of it
spent in writing, perhaps more of it spent in contesting a
power that suppressed what he had written. Carrying them
in a satchel, he peddled his own privately printed books.

He wrote his first book when he was less than thirty
years old but was considering himself "an old stove-up
cowpuncher." It is the story of his life on the range.
During the last twenty years or so of his life he repeatedly
rewrote the story, with the additions made by time but
without those extensions in meaning that an expanding intellect gives to a subject on which it prolongs consideration.
His second book, however, is independent of the first, beginning with his employment as a private detective in Chicago in 1886. Two years before this a blind phrenologist

75

who came to Caldwell, Kansas, had felt his "mule head" and assured him that he was "cut out for a detective." His titles in order of publication are: *A Texas Cowboy* (1885), *A Cowboy Detective* (1912), *Two Evil Isms: Pinkertonism and Anarchism* (1915), *A Lone Star Cowboy* (1919), *Billy the Kid* (1920), *Riata and Spurs* (1927). Siringo had five themes: his experience on the range; Billy the Kid, whom he chased as a cowboy; Pinkerton's National Detective Agency, for which he worked for twenty-two years; tough men and tough experiences that he met as a detective; and then more tough men. He had an inclination to write about women but suppressed it. Whatever he might have said on the subject would not have been news. His collection of cowboy songs is hardly to be rated as a book.

The first book of any significance pertaining to the range, *Historic Sketches of the Cattle Trade of the West and Southwest,* by Joseph G. McCoy, appeared in 1874. In point of time, Siringo's *A Texas Cowboy, or Fifteen Years on the Hurricane Deck of a Spanish Pony* was the second range book of any significance to appear. The next landmarks, in time, are Owen Wister's *The Virginian* (1902) and *The Log of a Cowboy,* by Andy Adams (1903). Since the beginning of the century many valid books, historical, semifictional, biographical and autobiographical, have been added to the literature of the range.

Siringo was not only the first authentic cowboy to publish an autobiography; of all cowboys, both spurious and authentic, who have recollected in print he was the most prolific in autobiographic variations. No record of cowboy life has supplanted his rollicky, reckless, realistic chronicle. The nearest competitor in the qualities mentioned is *We*

Pointed Them North, by Teddy Blue (E. C.) Abbott, put into writing by Helena Huntington Smith. This book tells more about a cowboy's private life with public women and is far better written, but it and all other cowboy reminiscences, including Siringo's own retellings, are supplements to the initial autobiography.

"Dear Charley," Will Rogers wrote to Siringo — and Siringo printed the letter on a self-addressed postcard to be filled out with an order for his *Riata and Spurs* —

Dear Charley: Somebody gave me the proof sheet of your new book, "Riata and Spurs." and wanted to know what I think of it. What I think of it? I think the same of it as I do the first cowboy book I ever read, "Fifteen Years on the Hurricane Deck of a Spanish Pony." Why, that was the Cowboy's Bible when I was growing up. I camped with a herd one night at the old LX Ranch, just north of Amarillo in '98, and they showed me an old forked tree where some old bronc had bucked you into. Why, that to us was like looking at the Shrine of Shakespeare to some of those "deep foreheads." . . . If you live to be a thousand years old you couldn't write a bad book about the Cowboys — the stuff they did might be bad, but you could tell it so well it would sound almost respectable.

The virtue of *Fifteen Years on the Hurricane Deck of a Spanish Pony* is that it was written and published without benefit of respectability. There is, in truth, something incongruous in the present artistic reprint of it, with this sophisticated essay appended. The bibliographical history of the book justifies calling it "the cowboys' Bible."

The first edition, clothbound, "Copyrighted by Chas. A. Siringo, Caldwell, Kans.," without date, bears the imprint of M. Umbdenstock & Co., Publishers, Chicago, Illinois,

77

1885. This edition, now scarcer than hen's teeth, was very limited. The second edition, also in cloth, printed without allusion to the first, "Copyrighted by Charles A. Siringo, 1886," appeared under the imprint of Siringo & Dobson, Publishers, Chicago, Ill., 1886. Through page 316 it is identical with the first edition, except for lack of one of the two colored frontispieces and for the change in publisher's name on the title page. But this second edition has thirty-one pages of "Addenda," an "Index to Addenda," and a dedication. The Addenda tells how to get rich and go broke in the cattle business and gives an unvarnished account of how brutish cowboys treat their horses.

About the time it was published, Siringo moved to Chicago, thence to ride the hurricane deck of his literary pony over a long and crooked trail. The date of the next publication of the book is difficult to fix. In 1893, using the original plates, but without colored frontispiece, the Eagle Publishing Company of Chicago brought out a clothbound edition. On the back strip of the binding of my copy of this printing, the name Rand McNally and Co. is stamped in gold. Judging from advertisements in the back of the book, the Eagle Publishing Company was a subsidiary. Carl Hertzog of El Paso owns a paperbound copy of the book, issued by Rand, McNally and Company, Chicago, that, though undated, he is certain was issued prior to the 1893 printing, certain letters showing the type to have been less worn, or "broken." This printing reproduces both colored illustrations of the 1885 edition. Before long, Rand McNally & Co. issued the book, using the original plates, as No. 56 in their Globe Library series.

In answer to a query, on August 16, 1935, Mr. B. B. Harvey, editor of the publishing division of the company, wrote me: "Our records date back only to 1901. Between that year and 1912, when our publication of the book was discontinued, we printed 98,000 copies." Presumably, the company printed many thousands of copies before 1901.

They were paperbacked and were sold by butcher-boys on trains. Some day the history of butcher-boys as purveyors of literature should be written. The butcher-boys were not to be deprived of one of their best sellers by Rand, McNally & Company's dropping it from their list. In 1914 copyright on it expired. Immediately thereafter the J. S. Ogilvie Publishing Company of 57 Rose Street, New York, had the book set up in small font type, printed on rotten paper with very narrow margins, bound in paper, and placed on sale at thirty-five cents a copy. At the back of this printing is added a six-page "Publisher's Note" calculated to inspire young men to travel on railroads to the Texas Panhandle to become cowboys. According to a letter from the company dated June 28, 1935, between 1914 and 1926, when the book was dropped from their list, they "printed and sold 58,000 copies."

In 1915 Siringo published the statement, in *Two Evil Isms,* that copies of the book "up into the hundreds of thousands" had been sold. In 1919 he prefaced *A Lone Star Cowboy* with these words: "This volume is to take the place of 'A Texas Cowboy,' the copyright of which has expired. Since its first publication, in 1885, nearly a million copies have been sold."

During a drouth and die-up of the eighties — before government aid to suffering citizens became popular —

some farm and ranch people in Jack County, Texas, gathered together to pray for rain and, in case it didn't rain, for supplies from the charitably inclined. Most provisions in those days came in barrels and were sold to ranches by the barrel. "Oh, God," an old cowman prayed, getting louder and higher as he proceeded, "soften the hearts of people in the East to send us according to our needs. Put it into their hearts to send us barrels of flour, barrels of lard, barrels of coffee, barrels of meal, barrels of salt pork, barrels of beans, barrels of molasses, barrels of sugar, barrels of vinegar, barrels of salt, barrels of pepper, barrels —" Just at this point his plea was broken into by an elbow against his ribs and a rough whisper, "Oh, hell, that's too much pepper."

"Nearly a million copies" of *A Texas Cowboy* is probably too much pepper. Range people have never been the chief consumers of any widely distributed book. *A Texas Cowboy* was widely distributed during forty years, under the imprint of five different publishers, and it is safe to say that, along with many readers who clerked in city stores and wanted to be cowboys, most men of the ranges who read at all read it. Many a ranch hand who had ridden a cattle train to Kansas City, Omaha, Chicago or some other market and then came back home in a chair car bought a copy of Charlie Siringo's book from the butcher-boy — provided also with *The Ashes of Love, Why Women Sin, A Wounded Heart, The Unmarried Mother, Custer's Last Fight,* and *Anna Karenina,* by Count Leo Tolstoi. Whatever the total number of copies printed, *A Texas Cowboy* has been, by far, Siringo's most-read book, also the most-read nonfiction book on cowboy life.

When Siringo rewrote the story of his boyhood and early manhood under the title of *A Lone Star Cowboy*, he left out many vivid incidents and cow camp phrases. It was this politer version that he transformed into *Riata and Spurs*. He had grown more cautious, and he seemed to have the idea that the public would be more interested in bad men than in his own personal experiences. Whisky-peet, or Whiskey-peat — under either spelling a mighty tough pony — seems to have more vitality than the Whisky Pete in the print of a Boston publisher. In *A Texas Cowboy* the dew is on the vine and vitality is uncurbed by correctness, discretion, decorum and other respectabilities. The young cowboy rides "with his head thrown back and a-singing a song." Instead of rashly writing down his own rashness, as he had done at thirty, Siringo, past sixty, in a field no longer "untrodden," was reviewing the rashness of another man. While he never lost altogether his youthful buoyancy, he did not possess that combination of spirit and imagination which for some men and women the years only enrich. Hudson at eighty put a richness into the story of his own *Far Away and Long Ago* youth that he could never have achieved while riding the pampas — on a Spanish cow pony that differed from Siringo's in surface brand rather than in breed.

Riata and Spurs is the meatier book, its parts more amply filled out, but Siringo the Elder makes no such quick judgments as in youth he made on certain cattle kings:

"Shanghai" Pierce and his brother Jonathan had sold out their interests . . . for the snug little sum of one hundred and ten thousand dollars. That shows what could be done in those days, with no capital, but with lots of cheek and a branding iron. The two Pierce's had come out there from Yankeedom a few years before poorer than skimmed milk . . . Mr. Grimes had a slaughter house on his ranch where he killed cattle for their hides and tallow — the meat he threw to the hogs . . . Did you ask kind reader, if those were all his own cattle that he butchered? If so, I will have to say that I never tell tales out of school.

Let us compare an account in (1) *A Texas Cowboy* with one of the same incident in (2) *Riata and Spurs*.

(1) An old Irishman by the name of "Hunky-dorey" Brown kept the store and did the settling up with the men. When he settled with me he laid all the money, in silver dollars, that I had earned since commencing work, which amounted to a few hundred dollars, out on the counter and then after eyeing me awhile, said: "Allen, Pool, & Co, owe you three hundred dollars," or whatever the amount was, "and you owe Allen, Pool & Co. two hundred ninety-nine dollars and a quarter, which leaves you seventy-five cents." He then raked all but six bits into the money drawer. . . . I thought the whole pile was mine and therefore had been figuring on the many purchases that I intended making. My intentions were to buy a herd of ponies and go to speculating. I had a dozen or two ponies, that I knew were for sale, already picked out. . . . After pocketing my six bits, I mounted "Fannie," a little mare that I had bought not long before, and struck out.

(2) I had been working for the Rancho Grande Company nearly two years, without a settlement or knowing how my account in the company store stood. My wages were twenty dollars a month, and whenever I needed cash all I had to do was ask old Hunkey Dory Brown, who was in charge of the store, for the amount, and he would charge it to my account. I was a surprised and disappointed boy when I found out I had only seventy-five cents to my credit.

This I blew in for a bottle of peaches and brandy and some stick candy before leaving the store to ride away on my own pony.

The latter account reports the incident in a spirited manner. The earlier one, to use a phrase out of an old cowboy toast, pictures it with "a glow and a glee."

That toast seems to belong here. An old trail driver who knew Charlie Siringo taught it to me in San Antonio the very day that Siringo died. We were in an upper chamber of a hotel, trail drivers milling in the lobby below us and dancing to the music of three fiddlers. I remember the date from the fact that on the train home next day I read in a newspaper an account of Siringo's death. The toast must be recited with eyes fixed on a glass of red likker held out in the right hand:

> Here's to the vinagaroon
>   that jumped on the centipede's back,
> He looked at him with a glow and a glee,
> And he said, "You poisonous son-of-a-bitch,
> If I don't get you, you'll get me."

Well, God save us all from ever becoming wholly discreet.

Degrees of honesty are observable in all human expression, but nowhere more patent than in autobiographical writing. The nearest to zero in honesty that any autobiography pertaining to the range has reached is Frank Harris's *My Reminiscences as a Cowboy,* a book significant for its worthlessness. Charlie Siringo never pretends; he is as free from trying to make effects as any man who writes about himself can be. His ignorance of rhetoric and his

83

indifference to what appeals to the public were aids to honesty. From the first form in which he set down his experiences until the final form, he remained uninfluenced by the feeling of most writers on the West that they must raise thunder over oceans of blood. He specialized in bad men, but their gunmanship is never theatrical. His style, especially his early style, cannot be called dignified, but it is informed with the innate dignity of honesty.

One coldish, misty December day, towards sundown, in the year 1931, I rode up to a ranch house on the San Bernard River, in Brazoria County, Texas. A white man of advanced years was out in a pen with three Negro cowboys. One of them, hatless and gray-headed, had matches curled up in his kinky hair. The smoke from his pipe was mingling with the steam from a sweaty horse he was unsaddling. I meant to ask the white man about that way of carrying matches, but when he told me that his name was Jim Keller* I remembered that Charlie Siringo had spoken of a Jim Keller who once loaned him a saddle horse. This was the man. We went inside the house to drink coffee and talk. Somehow what he told me lit up the Charlie Siringo of mavericks, mustangs, mossy-horned steers, fenceless coastal ranges, hide and tallow factories and Shanghai Pierce's bellowing voice more than anything else I have met outside of Siringo's first autobiography.

Keller had known Siringo as a boy and worked with him on Grimes's Rancho Grande. "His father was Italian and his mother's name was Bridget. He was happy-go-lucky and usually out of luck. He could let more horses get away

* James W. Keller, 1850–1946.

with the saddle on than any other cowboy in the country. That first book of his told things just like they was."

Keller said Siringo was the most fearless and the coolest man he ever knew. One time on a cow-work Siringo and a cowboy named Otto had a quarrel. Soon afterwards Siringo was in camp squatted down on the ground eating dinner when Otto suddenly called out to him from behind, "Charlie, I'm going to kill you. Don't move."

Siringo turned his head just enough to see the barrel of a six-shooter.

"All right," he said, not interrupting eating on a calf rib, "but I have a favor to ask before I die."

"What is it?"

"You've heard me say more than once that I hoped I'd not die hungry. I dread dying on an empty belly."

Without saying anything but still holding his six-shooter on the target, Otto apparently agreed to let Charlie finish his last meal. Charlie did not seem to slow down the process of filling up on beans, calf ribs and skillet bread in order to put off the act of dying.

"And I have another favor to ask," Charlie went on, his back to Otto, his squatting position unshifted.

"What's that?"

"When you shoot, don't quit till you've killed me dead. Don't just wound me and leave me wallering around to bother other people. Even if you have to reload to finish me, keep on shooting."

Meanwhile, out of Otto's sight, Charlie's hand was deftly working towards his own six-shooter, which he wore frontward. In a flash it was out and Charlie whirled around, covering Otto.

"Otto," he called, "put that gun up. It might go off and shoot a horse or something. Put it up and eat your dinner."

Otto put it up and ate his dinner. As Jim Keller concluded the story, "A man's wrath cools on a full stomach."

Nobody would ever classify Siringo as an intellectual, but he had one quality of the thorough intellectual — freedom from sentimentality. As their songs, frequently wailing through calf slobber, testify, cowboys in general were inclined to be sentimental. Charlie Siringo certainly had affections, but his emotions were always controlled. May D. Rhodes heard him tell Gene Rhodes that he deserved no credit for the bravery attributed to him, that he was born without a sense of fear.

Without sentiment, he related experiences with a concrete fidelity and a remarkable economy, often with a quick humor and, especially in early years, with lightheartedness. Although he had a strong sense of justice, he was generally as objective towards the criminals he spent so many years pursuing as he was towards some stray cow shot down for her hide. He seems, for instance, to have cared not at all whether Billy the Kid, who pervades his narratives, was captured or not. Probably he sympathized with him.*

* The happy-go-lucky, improvident, haphazard expedition after Billy the Kid has more than anything else that he wrote about put Siringo's name into books — books that go on mulling over the career of "the Robin Hood of New Mexico." In literary qualities, most of this literature approaches the old Robin Hood ballads and folk tales about as nearly as some self-advertised "Athens of Texas" approaches the Athens of Pericles and Socrates.

The best man who rode with Siringo after Billy the Kid was Jim East. The clearest and most orderly account of the expedition to be found is in an essay by J. Evetts Haley: "Jim East — Trail Hand and Cowboy," in the *Panhandle Plains Historical Review*, Canyon, Texas, Vol. IV (1931). Haley also contributed a compact biography of Siringo to the *Dictionary of American Biography*.

What urged Siringo to write the story of a cowboy's life, and then go on and on rewriting it? It was not that "obscure, inner necessity" that Conrad felt driving him on. Siringo was not, like Thoreau, trying to "drive life into a corner" and squeeze out its meaning. He seldom so much as alluded to the realities within himself. As a writer he ignored those passions, those searchings for something essential, those vague yearnings, fears and hidings, those dreams that lie dormant and that smoulder and surge deep within the intelligent being. He wrote down only what a camera or a public stenographer might record. He recorded what the eyes and the memory of a first-class detective gave him. A large proportion of his books have to do with crime and violence, but it would never have occurred to him to speculate on "Murder as a Fine Art." The stuff of poetry, "emotion recollected in tranquillity," did not enter his reminiscences. He was singularly wanting in sensitiveness to the beautiful.

The most original pages Siringo ever published are the three that compose the preface to *A Texas Cowboy*. Playfully, but none the less truthfully, he there tells why he wrote not only this book but all the simulacra that followed: "Money — and lots of it."

In this preface — as original but not so blatant as David Crockett's preface to his autobiography — Siringo specifies the exact experience that set him to hunting and then to writing about an "untrodden field." It was the *Police Gazette,* imposed on a cow camp by two young Texans who could read only the pictures. The one other literary allusion that I have noticed in Siringo's writings is to "a finely-bound novel" that Billy the Kid gave him in exchange for a cigar-holder. He particularized on the "new ten-dollar cigar-holder," but leaves the novel as unidentified as the songs the Sirens sang to Ulysses. In April, 1940, Dawson's Book Shop, one of the most civilized institutions of Los Angeles, issued a catalogue listing sixteen books from Siringo's "Den." They are nearly all old acquaintances of mine — John W. Poe's *Billy the Kid,* J. L. Hill's *The End of the Cattle Trail,* Frank S. Millard's *A Cowpuncher of the Pecos* — for which I got the printer not to change spelling, punctuation or sentence structure. Not one of the sixteen books could be classed as literature in the restricted sense of the word.

Siringo was educated to the extent of being able to "read, write and recollect." Had his mind been permeated with the essence of literature, he would not have been the representative that he was of cowboys bookless and booted who rode so free over the free ranges. Agnes Morley Cleaveland, in her delightful *No Life for a Lady,* quotes a cowboy as saying, "I never read a-tall, 'cept when I don't want to think, which ain't often." But even nonreading cowboys, as a part of vacuum-abhorring nature, sometimes craved printed words. In the absence of something else, they not only read but memorized and recited the printing on tin can labels, sometimes arguing whether ozs. should be pronounced "ozzes" or "ounces." In *The Log of a Cowboy,* Andy Adams pictures such a literary session after supper one evening on the cattle trail to Montana.

Bob Blades toyed with the empty can in mingled admiration and disgust over a picture on the paper label. It was a supper scene, every figure wearing full dress. "Now that's General Grant," he said, pointing with his finger, "and this is Tom Ochiltree. I can't quite make out this other duck, but I reckon he's some big auger — a senator or governor, maybe. Them old girls have got their gall with them. That style of dress is what you call *lo* and *behold*. The whole passel ought to be ashamed. And they seem to be enjoying themselves, too."

Many a cowhand batching alone in some ranch outpost, a wooden shack or a dugout, was educated as to what the world was buying and using by a mail-order catalogue. After the big catalogues began circulating widely, they were probably read on the ranges more eagerly than the Bible was.

One cowboy of open-range days used to say that the most satisfactory reading he had ever done was in an abandoned nester's shack where he spent the winter. The nester's wife had papered the walls and ceiling of the one room with pages from a semiweekly newspaper and a farm journal. This cowboy started in on the south wall and read in turn the east, west and north walls and was well along on the ceiling when word from headquarters came for him to join the spring roundup.

While camping in the Cherokee Strip of Oklahoma about 1880, Dennis Collins, a beef buyer, sent his solitary helper to Dodge City on an eight- or ten-day trip with "strict orders not to forget to bring something to read." There was nothing readable at hand, Dennis Collins wrote long afterwards, "except a patent medicine pamphlet, and I had read that so often and so thoroughly that I had some of the symptoms of seven different maladies that were therein pronounced fatal. If I had been in the neighborhood of a drug store at the time, I should have bought a supply of the cure-all, regardless of results."*

Granville Stuart, who of all chroniclers among pioneer cowmen had perhaps the most richly stored mind, tells in his *Forty Years on the Frontier* a graphic story of book hunger. This was in 1860, twenty years before the library of his Montana ranch home was stocked with three thousand books, along with magazines and newspapers, all at the disposal of range men.

"My brother James and I were both great readers," he wrote,

and we had been all winter without so much as an almanac to look at. We were famished for something to read when some Indians from the Bitter Root told us that a white man had come up from below with a trunk full of books and was camped with all that wealth in Bitter Root valley. On receipt of these glad tidings, we saddled our horses and, putting our blankets and some dried meat for food on a pack horse, started for those books, a hundred and fifty miles away, without a house or anybody on the route and with three dangerous rivers to cross, the Big Blackfoot, the Hell Gate, and the Bitter Root. As the spring rise had not yet begun, by careful searchings we found fords on these rivers, but they were dangerous and at times we were almost swept away.

Arriving in the Bitter Root valley, we learned that the man who brought the books had gone back to the lower country but had left the precious trunk in charge of a man named Henry Brooks. We finally found him living in a tepee on Sweathouse Creek. We gradually and diplomatically approached the subject of books, and "our hearts were on the ground" when Brooks told us that Neil McArthur, a Hudson's Bay Company trader, who left the books in his care, told him to keep them until he returned. He gave him no

* Dennis Collins, *The Indians' Last Fight, or the Dull Knife Raid* (Girard, Kansas: Press of the Appeal to Reason, n.d.), p. 103.

authority to sell any of them. We told him how long we had been
without anything to read and how we had ridden many days, seeking
that trunk, and that we would take all the blame and would make
good with McArthur when he returned. At last we won him over,
and he agreed to let us have five books, for five dollars each, and if
McArthur was not satisfied we were to pay him more.

How we feasted our eyes on those books! We could hardly make
up our minds which ones to choose, but we finally settled upon
Shakespeare and Byron, both fine illustrated editions, Headley's
Napoleon and His Marshals, a Bible in French, and Adam Smith's
Wealth of Nations. After paying for them we had just twenty-five
dollars left, but then we had the blessed books, which we packed
carefully in our blankets, and joyfully started on our return ride of
a hundred and fifty miles. Many were the happy hours we spent
reading those books, and I have them yet [about fifty years later] —
all except the *Wealth of Nations,* which, being loose in the binding,
has gradually disappeared until only a few fragments remain. Mc-
Arthur never returned to the Bitter Root valley, and I do not know
what became of the rest of the books, but I do hope they gave as
much pleasure to some others as did the five to Brother James and
myself.

One of Granville Stuart's fellow cowmen didn't think
much of his passion for books. He bought a herd of cattle,
as he told, from Stuart to be delivered across country at
the railroad. Both buyer and seller went with the herd.

Granville was always a great hand to read. He thought it would
be a good thing to take a lot of books along for cowpuncher enjoyment. Darned if I know how many he had, but anyway a sackful.
The way those cowboys would tackle the books was a caution. They
would ride into camp and pick up a book and the cook could holler
"Grub Pile" till he was red in the face and never get all of them to
eat at the same time. As soon as one cowboy dropped a book, another
would grab it. The cook called me aside one day and told me he was

going to quit as the boys thought more of Granville's books than they did of his grub. It would not do to lose a good cook on the trail. I told him not to say anything and I would see that the books caused him no more trouble. The next day when we got to the Yellowstone, I gathered up the books and threw them into the river, thus starting the first circulating library in Montana.*

There were not many cowboys like John W. Kendrick, who became Wyoming's best-known senator and who, while the rest of the cowboys were playing poker, "was always to be found in his bunk with a book in his hand." The outstanding cowboy reader was Eugene Manlove Rhodes. He read not only in camp but on horseback, habitually carrying a book in saddle pocket or coat pocket. His fictional cowboys are as apt as he was in literary allusion, and in *Bransford in Arcadia* he explains this aptitude by saying that all cowboys smoked Bull Durham tobacco, got from each sack of tobacco a coupon valid for one paperbound book, and sent for the book. There were "three hundred and three" titles on the list, most of them classics, since not being copyrighted makes classics cheap. "The books were read," Gene Rhodes says.

Rhodes lived in New Mexico, but there were far more reading men on the ranges of the Northwest than of the Southwest. More young men with cultural backgrounds from New England, England and Scotland went to Montana, Wyoming and the Dakotas to ranch than to Texas and other parts of the Southwest. "Frank and I have gone in for a course in Shakespeare this winter . . . but Jem sticks to his Tennyson and such lighter stuff," wrote "I. R."

* A. J. Noyes, *In the Land of the Chinook, or The Story of Blaine County* (Helena, Montana, 1917), p. 50.

in a little-known little book entitled *A Lady's Ranche Life in Montana* (London, 1887). Frank had been in the West some time, but as a bride I. R. and her Jem had just come over from Kensington Gardens. One of Frank's literary experiences in the country would have been utterly foreign to the Staked Plains or the Mexican borders.

Riding alone on a horse-buying expedition, he was arrested by vigilantes for a horse thief and taken to a cow camp, the cowboys of which at once prepared to hang him. He protested his innocence, but evidence was incontrovertible that his horse was of the size and color ridden by a thief known to be on the dodge. A well-educated man among the vigilantes took the lead in cross-examining him.

"Where were you in 1881?" he asked.

"In Canada."

"Where were you in 1880?"

"In Montana."

"Well, where were you in 1879?"

"In Oxford University."

A derisive cheer followed this reply. He was weather-tanned and unshaven and wore rough clothes. "Tell that to the marines," came calls.

"I'm telling you. Give me time and I can prove it," Frank said.

The cross-examiner went on. "All right, name some authors you studied in Oxford."

"Livy, Virgil, Homer, Aeschylus, Euripides and. . . ."

The looks on the faces of the committee were changing. Breaking into the roll call, the cross-examiner said, "Quote some Latin and you are a free man."

"Propria quae maribus," he began and then translated the Latin into Greek. He was a free man.

Phillip Ashton Rollins, whose *The Cowboy* is the fullest exposition on the subject printed, whose magnificent collection of Western books and pamphlets, including saddle catalogues, has been presented to Princeton University, and who will go to his grave a romantic, said:

> The Englishmen brought a lot of culture into the West. There were practically no books out there, but an Englishman always brought Shakespeare with him: it was the decent thing to do. And they read their books, read them aloud to the cowboys, many of whom never got any further in their schooling than the rudiments of reading and writing. I've seen a bunch of cowboys sitting on their spurs listening with absolute silence and concentration while somebody read aloud. . . . Once when something of Oscar Wilde's was being read, one of the cowboys got up and left the room. Later I asked him why, and he said, "I don't see no beauty in watching a hog eat swill." And I remember once after we'd been listening to *Julius Caesar,* one of them said to me, "That Shakespeare is the only poet I've ever heard who was fed on raw meat." When I sold my ranch in Montana, I divided my books among the riders, and eighteen out of twenty-one wanted Shakespeare. I sent out fifteen sets of Shakespeare that year.*

In a privately printed — beautifully printed it is — autobiography entitled *Dakota Days* by Edson C. Dayton, who after ranching in North Dakota during the eighties and nineties returned to his gracious homeland in western New York, I find estimates of Milton's poetry and Gladstone's character. Dayton speaks of the "intellectual face" of a certain Dakota man. Watching the features of his

---

* Esther Felt Bentley, "A Conversation with Mr. Rollins," *The Princeton University Library Chronicle,* IX, No. 4 (June, 1948), 189.

young range manager "aglow with pride" in a pair of buggy horses behind which they were riding, he remembered these lines from a college classmate's poem:

> I have some kinship with the bee,
> I am boon brother with the tree;
> The breathing earth is part of me.

No such quality of intellect and spirit is expressed in the autobiographic literature of the range south of 36.

It is moralistic reading, insofar as reading of any kind is recalled, that cowboy chroniclers of the Southwest record. One day in 1885 while Frank S. Gray and his mother were sitting on the front porch of their ranch home in San Saba County, Texas,

an old man drove up in a buggy. He hitched his horse to the rack and came in carrying a heavy box and unpacked a fine assortment of Bibles. He had prayer books, hymns, psalms, concordances and Bible dictionaries, most of them bound in flexible morocco and illustrated. It was about noon, and Mother asked the old man to take out his horse and feed him while she prepared dinner. When I brought in the wood for the kitchen fire, she said, "Frank, I would be pleased if you would get some of those religious books." Since I was rambling around, she said she would not ask me to read the entire Bible but to buy the four gospels, Matthew, Mark, Luke and John, and study them.

After the old peddler had returned thanks at the table, he told us that he was a superannuated minister of the gospel now saving lost sheep by providing them with Christian literature. When we finished our meal, I, more to gratify my mother's wish than my own desire, bought the four little gospels in flexible leather. I took them back with me to Edwards County [where my brothers and I had started a ranch] and there read them. As my mother had said, they gave me a correct idea of the Christian religion. The other boys in the monotonous bachelors' cow camp, not having anything else to read, read them also.*

The autobiographic literature of the range may be classified into two categories: civilized and uncivilized, though there are shadings of both. I have gone through a long list of titles and picked out twelve that reflect cultivated minds and civilized perspective. They are: *My Life on the Range,* by John Clay; *Cattle, Horses and Men,* by John Culley; *Some Recollections of a Western Ranchman,* by William French; *A Ranchman's Recollections,* by Frank S. Hastings; *The Great Western Trail,* by Clinton Parks Lampman; *Ranching with Roosevelt,* by Lincoln A. Lang; *Cow Range and Hunting Trail,* by Malcolm S. Mackay; *Ranch Life and the Hunting Trail,* by Theodore Roosevelt; *Bucking the Sagebrush,* by Charles J. Stedman; *Forty Years on the Frontier,* by Granville Stuart; *A Tenderfoot in Colorado,* along with *The Tenderfoot in New Mexico,* both of them by R. B. Townshend.

The eleven writers of these books were all landowners as well as men of education. Not one of them was native to the range or a hired hand, as was Siringo. Hastings, the only Texan — by adoption — in the group, managed a big plains outfit that was owned in New York. Four of the writers were British. The vast coast and brush ranges of Texas that during a swift quarter of a century sent millions of longhorn cattle north clear to the Plains of Alberta, and with them a few thousand cowboys who stamped their type upon the whole Western cow country, are not repre-

---

* Frank S. Gray, *Pioneering in Southwest Texas* (Austin, Texas, 1949), pp. 145–46.

sented by a single autobiographer that can be called civilized.

The varied recollections assembled by George W. Saunders into two volumes called *The Trail Drivers of Texas* and the separately published recollections of Jack Potter, Frank Millard, Bob Lauderdale, Charlie Siringo and other men of the original cow country of Texas are rawhide in nature. They are bedrock history. They tell much, but because of a lack of that perspective which gives the writer a sense of values, they often miss much.

Curious as to what congeniality towards book-writing the rollicky young "stove-up cowpuncher" might have found in Caldwell, Kansas, where he was writing the story of his life in 1884, and as to what impression his book when published might have made on his neighbors, I ran through the files of Caldwell newspapers (weeklies) preserved in the excellent library of the Kansas State Historical Society at Topeka.

As a "merchant" in Caldwell from the fall of 1883 to the spring of 1886, Siringo believed in advertising as well as in himself. "Charlie Siringo," one of the paid-for local items went, "wants every cowpuncher, nester and Chinaman in the United States to know that he makes a specialty of fine cigars and tobacco." On June 5, 1884, the *Caldwell Standard* notified the public that "Charlie Siringo has opened his ice cream parlor and is now prepared to serve ice cream and cake, lemonade, and confectionaries and fruits of all kinds at almost any hour of the day or night." The *Caldwell Journal* of February 19, 1885, advertises Siringo and Pruyne's "Oyster Parlor, where you can get a good lunch, with a hot cup of coffee — none of your weak jim-crow stuff, but genuine cowpuncher coffee that will almost stand alone — thrown in."

There was a bookstore in town, selling things besides books. Among articles on the cattle drives, "Texas fever," wire cutting killings, rattlesnake cures and many other frontier subjects, the Caldwell papers occasionally printed discussions of books, Thackeray's novels and Carlyle's *Frederick the Great* among others. An account of Joseph E. Badger, Jr., living at Frankfort, Kansas, probably interested Siringo particularly. Joseph E. Badger, Jr., was writing five-and-ten-cent novels for Beadle, getting $100 for a five-cent novel and $200 for a ten-cent novel. It took him two weeks to write a novel, though Colonel Prentiss Ingraham could turn out one in twenty-four hours.

The editor of the *Caldwell Journal* evidently believed that the reading public was interested in cowboys, for he reprinted from New York and Chicago papers articles about "The Real Cow Boy" and a satire on cowboy singing to cattle. Immediately after word came that Henry Brown, marshal of Caldwell, had been killed at Medicine Lodge, Kansas, while attempting to rob a bank, the *Standard* issued an extra, May 8, 1884. Brown had for a time been a member of Billy the Kid's gang. The *Standard* secured a statement from Charlie Siringo detailing Brown's career. Siringo carried the dossiers of a thousand men in his mind. The *Standard* also published a "Sketch of Billy the Kid's Life," written by "one of the most respectable men in Sumner County, who led a party to assist in the capture of the Kid and who was on his trail when Pat Garrett killed him." This "respectable" citizen could have been none other than Siringo. The sketch, about three hundred words in length and very succinct, was probably the first piece of his writing to get into print. I don't know just when Siringo began writing *A Texas Cowboy* — with Billy the Kid in it — but it could hardly have been later than 1884.

On September 17 and again on September 24, 1885, the *Journal* printed in large type this notice: "New Book. A Texas Cowboy, or Fifteen Years on the Hurricane Deck of a Spanish Pony. Watch for its announcement shortly." On October 8, the announcement came. Charles A. Siringo, according to it,

has drifted over the ranges of Texas, Indian Territory, Kansas, New Mexico and parts of Old Mexico ever since the spring of 1867. The book is now in press and will be sold only by subscription. Order early, as there are only a limited number of copies in the forthcoming edition. Price $1.00. Address the publishers, M. Umbdenstock & Co., 134 Madison Street, Chicago, Illinois. For an agency, write to the author at Caldwell, Kansas."

On December 24, 1885, the *Journal* printed a one-paragraph review, as follows:

The latest book that has come to our table is Chas. A. Siringo's "Texas Cowboy." The story is that of a boy without a home, thrown upon his own resources to rustle a living out of the world. Mr. Siringo's style of narrative is better than one would expect from the chances he has had. He writes easily, and in language that all can understand. We, in reviewing the book, have learned many new things concerning the way the cattle business was conducted in the early days of that industry in the Southwest. It appears that the "Mavericking" business after the close of the war was about the leading industry; and all it took then to make a cattle king of one's self was gall and a good branding iron. Having worked for most of the early cattle kings and drovers of Southern Texas, Mr. Siringo in very plain language shows up the methods of increasing herds that were in vogue in those days. If the book had been condensed one fourth it would have given more general satisfaction to those who wish to learn of the early days of the cattle industry; but to the great reading public it will give far better satisfaction than the works of young authors usually do.

The *Journal* was a little pink, as would be said these days, on the subject of "cattle kings." There were many more sodhouse nesters in the country — and the kings of finance had not yet taken over the country's newspapers, even country weeklies. It was not nearly so pink as the *Oklahoma War Chief,* which stood militantly for "homes for the homeless and land for the landless," especially land in the Cherokee Strip, and which boiled with antipathy against "cattle barons" and preached the philosophy of Henry George. As a civic booster, Siringo helped move the Oklahoma Boomers and their *War Chief* to Caldwell about the time he was leaving for Chicago — and the Pinkertons.

Pinkerton's National Detective Agency was both rain and drouth to Siringo as a writer. For twenty-two years he was a detective in the pay of the agency and, in his own words, was during all that time gathering "material for a second volume." By 1910 he had written the book on his experiences as a detective. From then until the end of his life the agency blocked him and kept the "tiger blood" in him boiling. For two years publication of his *Pinkerton's Cowboy Detective* was held up in the Superior Court of Chicago — until he changed the title to *A Cowboy Detective,* changed the name of Pinkerton's National Detective Agency to Dickenson Detective Agency, substituted other fictitious names, and cut out a good deal of material. The agency's protests were "undoubtedly rightful," Siringo's hand wrote in the preface to *A Cowboy Detective* as published (1912).* Conscience — long delayed — and "tiger blood" did not say so, however. Three years later Siringo published in Chicago, under the nose of Pinkerton's National Detective Agency headquarters, exactly what he felt concerning "the most corrupt institution of the century." The agency probably surmised that to take public action against *Two Evil Isms: Pinkertonism and Anarchism* would spread its views; the agency did nothing, and the slight book seems to have done nothing.

More than anything else that Siringo wrote, however, this book reveals the workings of his matured mind towards society. In the beginning, his sympathies were with labor, and it was only when he saw anarchists betraying labor that he sought a job with Pinkerton's to bring them to justice. Very soon his eyes were opened. The falsities in reports about anarchists made by agency men "would make a decent man's blood boil." Perjured testimony, "third degree" brutality and padded expense accounts were other agency evils that he felt — after long delay — called upon to expose. In *A Cowboy Detective* he called Tom Horn, of the Johnson County War fame, in Wyoming, "Tim Corn" and said that he was working for "private parties." In *Two Evil Isms* he boldly says that Horn was hired by the agency to help "wealthy cattlemen get rid of small ranchmen" at six hundred dollars a head. The latest biography of Tom Horn corroborates the statement. Siringo's

* In 1914 reprinted from same plates, at Santa Fe. This was handwritten in the book — an addition by JFD.

101

years of sleuthing left "one dark blot" on his conscience. That was his work against coal miners in their fight to wring justice from "greedy corporations." Not all the books concerning the Haymarket Riots, which initiated Siringo into his detective career, have yet been written; *Two Evil Isms* is a pointed source on the subject.

For years before *Riata and Spurs* appeared, in 1927, the dogs appeared to be sleeping. Now, vengeance in their voices, they opened up on Siringo again. Of the twenty chapters in his new book, eleven had been transposed, with revisions, from *A Cowboy Detective*. Actual names now took the place of the fictions that had been imposed by the Pinkertons. Among these actual names was that of Pinkerton's National Detective Agency, mentioned without criticism. There was nothing actionable in Siringo's use of their name, but the Pinkertons objected to his printing it. They bluffed the publishers into causing him to cut out about 150 pages relating his experiences as a detective and to substitute therefor material meant for another book to be entitled *Bad Men of the West*. This wholesale deletion and substitution made the second and subsequent printings of *Riata and Spurs* a very different book from the first, though no word of explanation in the second printing so indicates.

I never saw Charlie Siringo. I was not interested in him until about four years before his death. Really, I am not so much interested in him now as I was then. A matured sense of values tells me that it is much more important for more people to read *The Trial and Death of Socrates* than it is that anybody read *Fifteen Years on the Hurricane*

Deck of a Spanish Pony. However that may be, some details that Siringo left out of his self-portraits belong here.

Remembering him out of the days of the bloody Coeur d'Alene strike in Idaho, 1891–92, John Hays Hammond described him as "a slender, wiry man, dark-eyed, dark-moustached, modest. Lately recovered of smallpox, he was noticeably pitted. This would be an undisguisable identification in a tight place, but he did not seem to mind. . . . He was the most interesting, resourceful, courageous detective I ever dealt with."*

A lawyer who worked with Siringo in "the Mining War" and who wrote a book of reminiscences in which Siringo is the chief figure, thus describes him:

> He was deadly with a Colt's 45, a weapon he carried at all times. I have thrown up an empty bean can and watched him, shooting from the hip, riddle it in flight; yet he had never, so far as anyone knows, taken a human life. . . . He was shrewdly intelligent, infallible in his judgment of human nature, and courageous to the point of recklessness; he was quick and nervous normally, but in a critical moment, or an emergency, cold and steady as a rock. He was relentless on a scent. He was a rattler who never struck — a personality as interesting as any I have met along the frontier.†

Just before old Charlie was about to mount the pale horse and ride away into the dark, two writers of the West pictured him in such a way that the main features of their portraits might be undated. "A small man, weighing barely a hundred and thirty pounds, but wire-tough, brown of

---

* John Hays Hammond, "Strong Men of the West," *Scribner's Magazine,* February and March, 1925. In *The Autobiography of John Hays Hammond* (New York, 1925, I, 191–96) Hammond details the work of Siringo in the strikes, but does not describe him so specifically.
† William A. Stoll, *Silver Strike* (Boston, 1932), p. 183.

face, and keen of eye, with humor still invincible in spite of his seventy-two years," wrote Neil M. Clark.*

The next picture is from Siringo's old friend Gene Rhodes, the gallant.

Faded brown eyes, but sharp eyes that never miss the slightest movement of any person or anything. Not nervous but always alert. A thin face, brown like saddle leather; wind and sun have tanned that face beyond all changing. Most expressive hands; thumbs especially; thumbs which fill out and picture forth the story as he talks; a trigger finger that sticks out with every gesture. Fascinating forefinger. You can't take your eyes from it. Thin lipped; a mouth that would be hard if it were not for an occasional quirk of humor. Quite a frank smile, and often a chuckle. Not a tall man; slender — yes, frail. You note this with a shock; listening, not once had you thought of him as a small man or as an old one. A small head, a boy's head. And he is a boy, full of mischief and keen fun. Looks right at you when you talk, but always notices what anyone else happens to be doing. . . . Small feet. Corded throat. . . . Carries a loaded cane; polished steer-horn tips on a steel rod; probably made for him in a penitentiary. Wears a small red silk handkerchief, a low-crowned Stetson, neat clothing and shoes; not boots. Straight back; does not stoop; head carried like Chanticleer.†

Charlie Siringo had almost nothing to say on life; he reported actions. He put down something valid on a class of livers, as remote now from the Atomic Age as Rameses II. His cowboys and gunmen were not of Hollywood and folklore. He was an honest reporter.

* Neil M. Clark, "Close Calls: An Interview with Charles A. Siringo," *The American Magazine*, January, 1929. In this interview Neil Clark makes an intelligent interpretation of Siringo's philosophy on bad men — something missing in two articles purporting to be from "Letters of Charley Siringo," by Raymond D. Thorp, in *Western Sportsman*, Denver, Colorado, July and August, 1940.

† Eugene M. Rhodes, "He'll Make a Hand," *Sunset Magazine*, June, 1927.

Preface to "A Treasury of Western Folk-lore," edited by B. A. Botkin

ALL AUTHENTIC FOLKLORE represents authentically the folk to whom it pertains. Plain people — folks — seldom misrepresent their own nature. Their natures may be dull and asinine, but they talk like themselves and not like self-conscious, striving journalists. However false to documentary history, their traditions are true to social history.

Most Texans believe and all academic historians doubt the tradition that Travis drew a line in the besieged Alamo and invited whoever would die with him to cross it. All but two men stepped over the line; Bowie was carried over on his cot and the other exception escaped to tell the story. Whether true to fact or not, this story is true to the bravery, the desperation and the heroical ideals of the men of the Alamo. Some traditional tales about Jim Bowie's use of the Bowie knife are sheer inventions, but all of them express the Bowie knife culture that preceded six-shooter culture.

On the other hand, as examples of spurious folklore, a great many of the exaggerated yarns hitched onto David Crockett were manufactured by almanac-makers. The slick, glib language in which these yarns were printed was never used by Crockett or any other backwoodsman.

Most of the folklore of the Southwest deals with country things and ways: with nature in the form of drouths and thirst, duststorms, floods, northers, cyclones and the like; with animals, notable range horses, old-time longhorn cattle, coyotes, bears, rattlesnakes, roadrunners, jackrabbits, pack rats, tarantulas, centipedes, boll weevils, skunks and numerous other creatures; with certain plants, among them prickly pear, mesquite, mustang grape, cottonwood and the elusive "rattlesnake master weed"; with people themselves, both individuals and types that include the cowboy, bad man, sheepherder, muleskinner, homesteader, tenderfoot, miner and, of later times, wildcatter.

Perhaps the readiest way to judge whether the lore about these subjects is authentic or not is to measure its tempo. The tempo of the Southwest is compounded of the leisureliness of the Old South, the *mañana*-ness of Mexico and the waiting quality of the Indian. One driving slowly through certain parts of New Mexico and Arizona may spot an Indian up beside a rock looking away and away; if one halts to watch for movement by that Indian, he may have to wait until sundown. Genuine range people — among whom are not included oil millionaires who have bought ranches and hire somebody else to run them while they themselves operate in air-conditioned office buildings — have a limitless capacity for reserving their energy.

Their tempo has been so betrayed by Hollywood and Western, or "action," fiction that only the initiated know the truth. In this fiction, cowboys may "drawl" temporarily, but the medium to which they are condemned soon forces them to speak "in tense, grim tones." They almost never walk in the easy way that belongs to them and to cattle

106

that have just watered; instead of stepping through doors, they jump out of windows with six-shooter, often two six-shooters, blazing. One time while Dr. A. V. Kidder, famous archaeologist, was camped in a canyon in New Mexico excavating Indian ruins, he was awakened by shooting, yelling, the striking of iron hoofs on rocks, the beating of ropes on leather leggins (always called chaps in literature). He stepped out of his tent into the bright moonlight to investigate. Just then a cowboy he knew galloped up and halted.

"John," Dr. Kidder said, "what on earth is going on here?"

"Oh," John replied, "a damn fool named Zane Grey is paying us to make local color for him and we're doing our damndest to satisfy him."

I can see a cowman getting his hands out long before daylight and working until after dark for days and weeks, but during that stretch of time he misses his after-dinner nap. He lives in a land where shade is a blessing and where the sun is too intense to permit working with stock while it is at the zenith. I see this cowman sitting on his front gallery for hours at a time, day after day, watching the clouds or hoping for one, watching the dust from whirl-winds, listening to the summer sizz of locusts and observing other dry weather signs. He knows that spurring won't make it rain, and he has serious doubts on the power of prayer; he is as patient as a buzzard in waiting upon "the will of God." That is his tempo. His talk while he slowly swallows uncounted cups of coffee in his own kitchen or in a town cafe is in the same tempo.

In every motion picture I have ever seen showing a herd

of cattle they are kept moving at such a rate that no spectator can read their brands. Sitting through one of these pictures, a person who didn't know better would think that a trail herd of cattle bound for Montana from South Texas ran up the trail all day and stampeded sky-westward and crooked-eastward every night. Actually, they walked maybe ten miles a day, grazing a considerable part of the time and taking a long time to water out. Slow motion with stock is natural to stock people. The songs sung around herds on their bedgrounds were in tempo as slow and monotonous and doleful as camp meeting tunes designed to draw sinners to the mourners' bench.

> It's a whoop and a yea and a driving the dogies
> For camp is far away.
> It's a whoop and a yea, get along my little dogies,
> For Wyoming may be your new home.

If you listen to talk by men of the range tradition you will hear more about "moseying around" than about moving "like a bat out of hell." The good storyteller likes to linger in the shade, and his best stories have a lingering quality. Mark Twain developed his "Celebrated Jumping Frog of Calaveras County" from a folk anecdote. Actually, there is no jumping in it at all, not even frog-jumping; it is a tale of almost exasperating leisureliness about people who owned time.

The folklore of the Southwest, in common with that of other regions, has not been woven by people of worldly success. The only mines that amount to anything in this folklore are lost forever; the only money that figures in it is buried deeper than oil driller ever bored. What makes the tales of lost mines and buried treasure realistic does not lie in the tables of expectation that give fabulous profits to the life insurance business; it lies in the hope inspired by imaginations — an asset that no banker will honor. Success in business gives one kind of hope, but it is not the kind that keeps the Lost Dutchman, the Lost Bowie, the Lost Adams Diggings and many another fabled lode rich and alluring. "It is better to travel hopeful than to arrive," Robert Louis Stevenson said. The hunters and tellers of lost mines are the hopefuls, with time to spare.

The people who enriched the stockpile of world folklore with tales of a cottontail rabbit — tales that through the genius of Joel Chandler Harris are fastened permanently to Uncle Remus — were underdogs. In the Southwest, a great cycle of corresponding tales pertain to the much persecuted coyote. They have not come from owners of sheep, but from unpropertied Indians and Mexicans. These peoples have lingered with the grass, the rocks, the thorned shrubs and the chirping crickets. They have not spent their energies helping make America the most highly industrialized nation on earth. They have had time to fancy and imagine and have felt a kinship for their fellow creatures of the earth. To appreciate their contribution is not to deprecate industry, but enjoyment of the delightful may make the enjoyer skeptical of claims that "America's greatness" is based entirely on the enterprise of manufacturing corporations.

Of course, as even the most cursory examination of the present collection will show, a great deal of the folklore of the West grows out of hard realities. Some of it is as a

109

relief against realistic hardness. Read Hamlin Garland's illusionless stories on homesteader farming in the Middle West and know why there is almost no folklore of a romantic flavor connected with it in contrast to that connected with the cowboy's occupation. Ranching and dry-farming alike depend on rain and alike are ruined by drouth. No torture to men and their families can be more blasting than prolonged drouth. The tall tales about rains made of dust and of west winds so constant that they blow hell out of ambitious cyclones are but stiff upper lip gibes against fate. They do not express the Celtic "rebellion against fact"; they come from facing fact. They are materialistic in temper and defy the worst while facing it.

The westward movement that started with the discovery of gold in California and is still going on in drilling for oil miles under the surface of the Pacific Ocean and the Gulf of Mexico has been America's Elizabethan Age of spacious times and terrible toiling. The folklore that this Elizabethan Age of America generated has a reckless gusto and an energy peculiar to itself. It is not concerned with the soul as was New England folklore represented in Hawthorne's story of "The Minister's Black Veil." The long ago does not echo in it as in "Rip Van Winkle." It does not have the mellowness of people who have lived a long time in one place and expect to remain there. Indeed, it is in revolt against tradition. Its commonest form, perhaps, is the tall tale.

The tall tale, the tale that depends for its effect upon mathematical proportions, did not originate in America, but Americans have certainly made it their own. It lacks humanity — the humanity, for instance, of "Barbara

Allen." It does not spring out of cherishment for the object on which the tale is told. The Southwest has gone along with all other regions of the West in telling them tall, but the richest part of the folklore of the Southwest is not in this field. Mary Austin's "One Smoke Stories," which are Indian and Mexican, express, while not lacking irony, a harmony between the tellers and their subjects and a cherishment for those subjects. The folklore of the Southwest that has charm and humanity has grown out of a continuing way of life. There is plenty to say against the rigid conservatism of the Old South; but it is from settled ways of life — the Old South ways, the old rancher ways, the old Mexican ways, the old Indian ways — that folklore of charm and imagination comes. Ghosts do not haunt one-night camps.

The tall tale does not set imagination traveling into realms of human destiny. It lacks spiritual content. It is an aside from the materialistic, even metallic, way of American life. But it amuses. If it is not the product of troubadours who live where it is always afternoon, it is the product of people halted from the business of acquiring things. They have halted in repose to yarn, and their yarns express the take-your-time tempo that belongs to the land.

Austin, Texas

Jim Williams and
"Out Our Way"

ONE EVENING down in the Sierra Madre of Mexico I was camped with two *arrieros* — muleteers. They wore rawhide sandals. Neither could read a word printed in any language. Around the bend of the canyon trail we saw a man riding toward us, the first human being sighted during a day and a half of travel. He was on a fairly good bay horse.

"Look at that *rocinante*!" one of the *arrieros* exclaimed.

His use of the name of Don Quixote's steed, a name that has become a synonym for horse wherever Spanish is spoken, struck me as evidence of supreme fame.

In San Antonio a cowman of trail-driving days was packing me with lore about the old-time Texas longhorns, on which I was writing a book. He was describing how, after the railroad came, their heads had to be twisted around, on account of the horn-spread, for them to get through the loading chute and the door of a stockcar.

"I wish I had a picture of that," I said.

"I know where you can get it," he replied.

"Where?"

"Pasted up in the courthouse in Fort Stockton."

Fort Stockton is a ranch town west of the Pecos River.

112

The old cowman went on to say that the picture was a newspaper clipping, one of J. R. Williams's *Out Our Way* cartoons. He said he was going to be in Fort Stockton in about a month to receive some cattle and thought "the boys" would let him have the cartoon for use in a history of the longhorns. "It's been there a long time," he said. "It talks to a lot of us, but I think I can get it."

About a month later it came to me in a letter. . . . There the cowboys are, twisting the heads of the old mossyhorns so as to angle them into the cars. To them the business is altogether worrisome and not at all picturesque. On the gangplank stands a tramp. He is no doubt expecting a free ride to Kansas City or some other market on the cattle train. The mighty horns are not exactly picturesque to him either. They are a wonderment, however.

That tramp represents interest in the picture by people who have not lived the life. To every inheritor of the tradition of the range its homely vividness means something as personal as a plot of ripe mesquite grass on which a man unrolls his pallet and after dark listens to his horse comfortably grazing.

Jim Williams has never created a classic of *Don Quixote* fame, dateless and universal, but his characters, his mule, his horses, his cattle, his incidents, and the places where they are pictured talk to us with an easy naturalness. He has yearned to be a great artist. Some of his canvases, which few have seen, express conceptions of life and beauty beyond the reach of cartoons. He has always been genuine in those cartoons, however. Their humanity, humor and sincerity, and realistic details come home to people.

He has sometimes been criticized by indoors perfectionists for not having a buckle or a rope knot exact according to Hollywood rodeo specifications. To people who have heard the music of calf bawling, wished there were more grass and less rocks, and shifted a saddle pillow on the ground to keep the moonlight out of their eyes, the buckles and rope knots make little difference. These people catch the spirit, the reality of the pictures. The bodies of those old longhorns and of the blue ribbon whiteface calves, their supplanting opposites, would not, as Jim Williams draws them, serve as models for an art class studying anatomy. Yet they convey the idea, the impression, the situation — which is all that a cartoon is supposed to convey.

Jim Williams is a very diffident and humble man. He deprecates his own work with a modesty painful both to himself and his friends. He considers that he knows less about cows and cowboys than any other man who ever owned a ranch or led an outlaw out of a thicket. He was a cowboy in New Mexico and Arizona country where the only way to catch up with the sound of cattle tearing away is to tear a hole through the brush and somehow keep from being knocked off by this limb and jabbed through the groin by that one. He has owned and operated a forty-five-thousand-acre ranch, doing his own part of the work. He has cooked for cow outfits and put up with camp cooks in his own pay. He was a cavalryman for three years in the days when cavalry meant horses. Yet he will tell you very sincerely that he never had any range experience amounting to a hill of beans, that he has always been a poor observer, can't remember details, and would rather be taken for a horse thief than considered as posing as an authority on range life. Also, in his own words, he "would rather have been a fairly successful cowman out in the bright sunlight of the days than be the most successful cartoonist that ever lived." If giving his own shirt to any cowpuncher who came along would make a cowman successful, I imagine Jim Williams might have become the king of cattle kings.

He is sensitive in fine ways often to be read in the cartoons. Not long after he sold his ranch out from Prescott, Arizona, and moved to a big house in the woods of San Marino, California, he saw a coyote on his own grounds. It was just at dusk, and it was at dusk when he showed me the place where the coyote had stood, "as gant and lank" as a coyote ever was. In a minute he was gone, but that night Jim Williams put out a pan of grub for him. "I knew he'd never come back near that pan," he said, "but exiles do strange things. I'm one myself. I'm remembering how for sixteen years I killed coyotes. I feel different toward them here on the edge of a great city."

He likes to remember people and things that have appealed to him. That is one of the marks of a generous nature. I imagine that his continuing cartoons on the "Worry Wart" and "Why Mothers Get Gray" often trail back to the long, long thoughts as well as to the devilments of his own boyhood. The cartoons on the machine shop dominated by the "Bull of the Woods" go back to his work as a machinist. "Born Thirty Years Too Soon" has carried millions of people back to times before the horseless carriage machined the world.

James Robert Williams does not spend much time remembering that he was born in Nova Scotia, whence as a baby he was brought to Detroit. In his dreams he was born

115

in the time and place for driving longhorns up the trail from South Texas over a continent of unfenced grass to the plains of Montana — where Charles M. Russell, the artist he likes best, rode with the Blackfoot Indians. The *Out Our Way* cartoons depicting Curly and Stiffy, old hands, Wes, the young learner, Big Ick the Negro, and Sugar, the unpredictable cook, are his favorites. These characters and others associated with them come out of two deeply seated realities in their creator: his own experiences on the range and his dreams of a free life in the open. They express imagination even more than they express actuality. As imagined, they are more real than literal copies could ever be.

Over years of time Jim Williams has been living with these characters on their own spaces of mesa, mountain and canyon, with here and there a hole of alkalish water. It is manifest that he likes to linger with them. Being true to life, they like to linger also. They never have that "tense, grim tone" of the Zane Grey factories. In action they are habitually as easygoing as their humor, though when the time comes they can unlimber and sock the spurs. They and their kind are more congenial to the taste of Jim Williams than some important estate-holders.

The despair of any writer is not being able to say in a whole page of paragraphs what a skillful illustrator can say in a few lines. Take the cartoons of "The Rusty King." In the first place, he's smoking a pipe, which all authorities on cowboy life as depicted by cigarette and mail order advertisements say is never done on the range. His bridle reins are made of an old rope. His hat, if it did not leak, would hold about nine gallons and three quarts less than the orthodox Stetson. Instead of wearing boots, he's wearing shoes. The ignominious mare he straddles has cholla joints in her tail and is asleep on one hip while he sits sizing up a bunch of cattle that only cow people can see.

They are not visible in the picture. They're there, just beyond, all the same. And the Rusty King could tell what cow that bleating calf belongs to; he could tell the personal history of nearly every brand in the herd; he could make a pretty close guess at what the yearlings weigh now and what they'll weigh next spring if it rains, also what they'll weigh if it does not rain. He knows this herd has not been watered since yesterday morning, but he's not saying anything critical on the way they've been handled. He's a stingy old cuss — the kind who tells the cook to bake bread today for eating tomorrow, so the hands won't use up so much flour. He could write a check, all cow money, for a herd ten times as big as the one he's about to receive. If a day's drive from where he counts them one is missing, he will send some old stove-up cowpuncher back alone to find it, and he'll tell him in just what draw he's apt to find it.

Of course, Jim Williams does not placard all this. He merely placards a remark or two about the Rusty King. People who can't read what is not placarded don't know the untold. Yet they get the point. Those who can read the untold linger with delight on such pictures and remember.

I wish there were more of satire in *Out Our Way*. It is never caustic. No satirist with a voice as soft and a nature as winsome as Jim Williams's could be caustic. He is one of the gentlest gentlemen I have ever known. His satire is a placid, never contentious, sensible commentary not as much on range life as on city ideas — and the cartoonist never forgets that he is cartooning for people in cities back East. For instance, a cartoon shows Wes trying to take a colored movie of a cowboy pulling a cow out of a bog hole. A block of salt on the bank shows that this has been a good watering place, though it is now little but mud. Off to one side, the skull of a cow shows what disaster bog holes mean. A rope about the cow's horns, for about her neck it would choke her, is tied to the saddle horn on the cowboy's trained horse, and the horse is pulling back. Meanwhile the cowboy, old Curly, is heaving on the cow's tail, raising her all he can.

Why, a picture of a cowboy working, Curly says, "would spoil all the glamour and romance. Never tak 'em doing anything but galloping, shooting and leaning up agin a bar."

According to biographical sketches, Jim Williams left school when he was fifteen. He reads the best of literature, including poetry. His library is well stocked with Western books. He once took a short course in drawing. He had knocked around the world a lot and had practiced drawing many cartoons before NEA Service Inc., one of the largest syndicates in the world, saw one that it liked. For twenty-nine years now he has been publishing a cartoon every day in hundreds of newspapers. He may spend a day searching for an idea that he can put in black and white in a fraction of an hour. To vast numbers of people he is a part of their daily bread.

The cartoons in this book are merely selected samples in one field of his several subjects. They talk to us.

Captain Cook's Place
Among Reminiscencers
of the West

THERE MAY BE A FEW EXCEPTIONS — depending upon definition — but as a rule the most illuminating and, to civilized taste, the most readable personal narratives of the West have been written by men with perspective. This is especially true of narratives dealing with life on cattle range and trail. Writers of the best ones have been aware of life and values far away from their own camps and cows. Granville Stuart, called "the Father of Montana," whose *Forty Years on the Frontier* is primary on both early mining and ranching, had a thousand books in his ranch home and had read them. Edson C. Dayton's *Dakota Days, 1886–1898* (privately printed in 1937 and little known) has the word "intellectual" on page 2 and in describing a man's harmony with his horses quotes:

> I have some kinship with the bee,
> I am boon brother with the tree;
> The breathing earth is part of me.

Drunk on "shoot-'em-up" banalities, collectors have been strangely neglectful of John Culley's *Cattle, Horses and Men;* Culley was an Oxford man who ranched in New

119

Mexico, and when I went to see him after he had retired in California, he showed me a presentation copy of Walter Pater's *Essay on Style*. Montague Stevens, another New Mexico rancher from England, a Cambridge man, put into *Meet Mr. Grizzly* more about the sense of smell in animals than is found in any other book this side of W. H. Hudson's *A Hind in Richmond Park*. While I was writing *The Longhorns* I found more natural history about these cattle in R. B. Townshend's *A Tenderfoot in Colorado* than I found in the reminiscences of various native cowmen who had never been, mentally, away from cows. Nor has any gunman, directly or indirectly, recollected so delightfully of Billy the Kid as R. B. Townshend wrote about him in *The Tenderfoot in New Mexico*. Townshend came west from England to ranch soon after the close of the Civil War; he was a Cambridge man, and after many years of westering he returned to England and translated Tacitus under the spires of Oxford.

Perspective implies knowing what to look for in an object as well as a sense of relative values. Violence, exaggerated in fact and more exaggerated in tradition, has prevented many actors on the Western scene from seeing beyond violence itself. The average old-timer of open range days put himself wherever possible, and often where not possible, into Indian fights and stampedes and strained his memory to be an eyewitness to bad-man exploits. Professional sensationalists early made the labels for everything supposed to be interesting about the Old West; violence, danger, and climactic action composed about everything. Thereafter the great majority of Western men who came to chronicle their life experiences tended to slur

120

over anything for which there was not a label — printed in red and marked EXPLOSIVE. Cattlemen have probably lost a thousand times more cattle to screwworms than to cow thieves, but cow thieves have received more than a thousand times as much attention. You will look in vain through range autobiographies for consideration of screwworms. They are as realistic as Poe's romanticized "Conqueror Worm" or as Hamlet's delineation of the "progress of a king through the guts of a beggar," but screwworms have never been labeled as a proper subject for range-life chronicles.

There is plenty of violence in *Fifty Years on the Old Frontier,* by James H. Cook. He could not have been true to the land and the livers upon it at the time he rode among them without revealing this violence, but he saw beyond it. He was born to the tradition of the sea and as a boy wanted to go down to the sea. In the Michigan of his first sixteen years he learned woodcraft, shopcraft, and the Bible, before he came to Texas a cowboy for to be. But the perspective in forming his memoirs seems to have been developed after he left Texas and became a professional hunter and guide in Wyoming and New Mexico. In *Longhorn Cowboy,* which he wrote and Howard R. Driggs doctored up, he says: "I took advantage of associations with men of learning to broaden my knowledge. I met Professors L. D. Cope and O. C. Marsh, two of the world's greatest naturalists, and assisted them in their researches. I was of help also to Professors Hayden and King. . . . Conversations with these scientists aroused a desire to learn more." By the time he came to write the chronicle of his adventures, his ranch at Agate

Springs, Nebraska, had been host to paleontologists, anthropologists and other scientists from many universities and museums. He could not write about brush popping as if he had known no other talk than that of oxen.

It is significant that Yale University published his book, in 1923. It has been out of print for years. Among valid reasons for reprinting it is the fact that it was the first book within the realm of range books to deal with the brush country of Texas. As author of the second book (1929), *A Vaquero of the Brush Country,* on this singular part of the cattle world, I was acutely conscious of Captain Cook's validity as well as priority. Since those days of the 1870's when he and his fellow *vaqueros* roped outlaw cattle at night on openings between thickets, the brush, despite modern treedozing, has increased, wild cattle still hide in it, and brush popping still demands techniques far removed from those of the plains cowboys, but no man now can experience the pristine wildness of the *brasada* during Jim Cook's youth. He alone of the brush hands of his time set it down.

"Cow Waddies and Cattle Trails," Part I of his book, has for me a freshness and richness not common in what follows. The abbreviated account of managing the WS Ranch in New Mexico is hardly so good as *Some Recollections of a Western Ranchman,* by William French, who took over managership of the WS Ranch in 1887, the year Cook left it. The hunting episodes lack the natural history content inherent in the best hunting literature. Yet not many cattlemen who fought Indians became foremost among the understanders of and friends to the Indians as Captain Cook became. For him, in memory, an Indian scrap could not be the high point of narrative. Taking together everything he wrote pertaining to Indians, one gets a sense of development towards mature-mindedness in the man and writer.

Sometimes in reading reminiscences one judges that the writer had done better by keeping a journal and publishing it instead of looking back through the aura of vanished time. I do not have this feeling towards *Fifty Years on the Old Frontier*. The matter seems better to me for having been sifted by time and looked at from the perspective of maturity. On January 27, 1942, in his eighty-fourth year, James H. Cook died at his ranch home at Agate Springs, or Agate, on the Niobrara River in Sioux County, Nebraska. His son Harold blends ranching and science in a way that throws light on history.

Foreword to "Sheep, Life on the South Dakota Range," by Archer B. Gilfillan

IN 1896, while the Democrats over most of the country were campaigning under William Jennings Bryan for silver and the Republicans in Wyoming were campaigning for wool, a Wyoming senator "noted for building wire fences on government land and taking everything in sight" made a speech in Cheyenne that, according to Frank Benton's *Cowboy Life on a Sidetrack,* began as follows:

Fellow sheepmen and what few other citizens there are in Wyoming, what's the matter with the sheep business? Have we deteriorated in the eyes of the world in the last two thousand years? Who writes poetry of the sheep and sheepherder of the present time? What artist puts priceless paintings on canvas of the sheep business today? Why, fellow sheepmen, in ancient times all the poetry that was written was of the shepherd and his flock, and in every palace, in the most conspicuous place, hung a picture of a tall shepherd with venerable beard and flowing locks, his serape thrown carelessly over his shoulder, a long crook in his hand, leading his sheep over the hill to some fresher pasture. And when the people saw the original of this painting [coming homeward] in the sunset glow, they cried, "Lo, behold the shepherd cometh." Now what do they say? This is what you hear: "Look at that lousy sheepherding scoundrel coming over the divide with his sheep. Boys, get your black masks and the wagon spokes."

The "boys" called upon were, of course, cowboys. According to prolific fiction, a part of their occupation was to club sheep to death, also the sheepherder unless he made tracks fast for another part of the country. In contests for grazing on public lands, to which neither had any legal rights, some cattlemen of the last century did violence to sheepmen and their property in scattered areas, but the physical conflicts were never extensive. Nowadays many ranchers run both sheep and cattle. The conflict has been and continues to be in the realm of popular appeal. If, in the Niagara of "Westerns" highlighting cowboys, both good and bad, of six-shooters and saddles, a single novel has been devoted to a sheepherder or a sheep owner, it has not come to my attention. What producer would think of making a movie with no more action than a herd of grazing sheep suggests? All he really wants of cattle is a stampede, all of horses a running fight between their riders. The idea of a screen drama embodying the spirit of a shepherd beside "still waters" would be as odd as a debate in the United States Senate over the intellectual fitness of a cabinet appointee.

In nonfiction books, sheep and sheep people have done better. Even so, hardly a dozen genuine books on the subject can be listed. On the other hand, a collector with some knowledge, money, and persistence can amass a thousand titles treating of cows, cow horses, trail drivers, cowboys, cowmen, and the vast cow country. Only one of them, a special study, treats of cow nature as intimately and extensively as Archer B. Gilfillan treats of sheep nature.

Civilized perspective, which includes a sense of values, is a requisite for any writer who would make on any subject, especially himself, a book judged valid by mature minds. Gilfillan had that perspective, coupled with a cultivated power of observation. He had read and had integrated the precious heritage of literature with personal experience. The habit of reflection gave meanings to what he experienced. He took pleasure, no doubt, in refining the conveyance of his knowledge, play of mind, humor, and charm. The result is as revealing of himself as it is informing on the sheep world, the two elements having almost inseparably penetrated each other.

Among cow country books are all kinds, some wise in perspective, some rich in knowledge, some delightful in style, also more than a few revelatory of presuming ignorance and egotism, as if a little cowboying could alone make a good book. Of the comparatively few books dealing with sheep and sheep people, not one expresses striving ignorance.

The percentage achieving high standard is remarkable. Foremost among them stands *The Flock,* by Mary Austin (Boston, 1906), a classic in insight, sympathies, and style. More personal and gossipy is Hughie Call's *Golden Fleece* (Boston, 1942); it integrates family life on a Montana ranch with the sheep industry. Two excellent books sum up the history of sheep, which includes related animal life, the land, and men. They are *The Golden Hoof,* by Winifred Kupper (New York, 1945), a truly delightful book, and *Shepherd's Empire,* by Charles Weyland Towne and Edward Norris Wentworth (University of Oklahoma Press, Norman, 1946), more extensive but not so much fun. All but the last-named are out of print. All four together have not sold as many copies as the first printing of one of Zane

Grey's novels woven around some range rider with a tense grim tone who if he is not shooting with two six-shooters at the same time is shooting with one.

Robert Maudslay came to Texas from England in time to drive flocks across the unfenced ranges of California, New Mexico, and Wyoming. He became both owner and herder of sheep. Like Archer Gilfillan, he lived a bachelor, speculated about women, and read books. Long after he retired from the sheep business he wrote his memoirs. The one personal narrative in the field worthy of a place beside Archer B. Gilfillan's *Sheep* is *Texas Sheepman: The Reminiscences of Robert Maudslay,* edited by Winifred Kupper — a niece with a sense of humor and with sheep in her education — (University of Texas Press, Austin, 1951). Thus, with the present reissue of *Sheep* by the University of Minnesota Press, the only three good books in print pertaining to the subject are made available by university presses. It seems almost obligatory that some university press bring Mary Austin's *The Flock* back into circulation.

Maudslay's favorite reading seems to have been all of Scott, all of Shakespeare, and the *Illustrated London News* throughout his life. "What could a man who read Shakespeare and the *Illustrated London News* contribute to Comey ti yi yoopeeyea, / Ti yi ya?"

An indefatigable singer of cowboy songs who claimed to have been a cowboy asserted to me once, in answer to a question: "No, the sheepmen never had any songs. They are not smart enough, I guess, to make them up." No orthodox cowboy, cowman, cowman's wife or daughter ever did consider any sheepherder, sheep rustler, or sheep owner smart enough to get in out of the rain. "Crazy as a sheepherder" is a traditional range expression, along with "crazy as a bedbug." "Do you know what makes sheep-herders go crazy?" One answer is, "Trying to figger out the long way from the short way of a boughten quilt." The other, and more common, is that they associate with no-body but sheep or, what is worse, themselves. This kind of folklore may have had something to do with public indif-ference in the United States to literature concerned with sheep and sheep people. If wide open spaces and a lone man on the lone prairie are desiderata for readers of litera-ture about the West, they are as inherent in sheep books as in cow books.

A few biographical facts about Archer B. Gilfillan are in place. He was born in 1886 on the White Earth Reserva-tion for Ojibway Indians in Minnesota, his father being a missionary there. When Archer was about fourteen, the family moved back East and he graduated with Phi Beta Kappa from the University of Pennsylvania. He had won prizes in writing but soon after graduation homesteaded in South Dakota. The land was hardly worth the time he spent "proving up" his claim. After various vicissitudes he settled down to herding sheep for wages for eighteen years — sixteen of them with one owner. It was at the insistence of his sister Emily Muriel Dean, to whom *Sheep* is dedi-cated, that he wrote the book. Some chapters were pub-lished in the *Atlantic Monthly* before Little, Brown and Company, of Boston, brought it out in October, 1929. For some years after giving up sheepherding Gilfillan was a roving newspaper writer. In 1936 he had a folio of his newspaper essays issued in paper covers at Custer, South Dakota, under the title of *A Shepherd's Holiday*. When he died in Deadwood, in December, 1955, his one real book had been out of print for a decade.

Henry David Thoreau's short-lived retreat to Walden Pond afforded a kind of philosophical precedent for Archer Gilfillan's long retreat into the short-grass country of northwestern South Dakota. He was not bent like Thoreau on "driving life into a corner" and analyzing it to the core, but he was just as set on being independent in all ways. The "all-pervading calm" of the land on which he lived alone in his sheepwagon brought to him "an interior peace." Herding sheep, instead of depressing him with monotony, interested him with variety. It gave him plenty of time to read, especially that individualist Samuel Pepys, and to escape having his time cluttered up with people and the things that ride mankind. It left him free to think his own thoughts and "to live his own life in his own way."

Fences have replaced shepherds on many sheep ranges; government trappers have destroyed coyotes and gray wolves so that they are no longer much of a hazard to flocks; but *Sheep* as delightful and informing reading has in nowise been made obsolete by the advent of the Atomic Age. The story of Three Toes, the most cunning of lobos, in the chapter called "The Herder's Neighbors," is as graphic as ever and more to be prized because it could not happen now. The philosophy of the man will go on making cheerful sense.

A dog named Bobbi "did not want to catch rabbits; all he wanted was to chase them, like the man who followed bear tracks all day and then quit them because they were getting too fresh." Concerning those persons of importance who upon touching the fringes of the cow country "deck

129

themselves out in full cowboy regalia, get in front of a camera and look tough," Gilfillan concluded: "Naturally the toggery does not make the celebrity a cowboy any more than a fringe of grass around his waist would make him a hula hula dancer, but a pleasing illusion to the contrary doubtless exists."

January 15, 1957

Captain John G. Bourke
as Soldier, Writer and Man

CAPTAIN JOHN G. BOURKE understood the Apache people and the Apache country. He knew the Apaches — also other tribesmen — as a soldier, as a scholar, and as a man with eager sympathies for nearly all things human except greed, fraud, and injustice, against which his righteous indignation burned until the fire of his own life went out.

While *An Apache Campaign* is an independent unit of writing, it illuminates and is illuminated by certain other works written by Bourke. It had been published serially in *Outing Magazine* in 1885 before it was issued as a book the next year by Charles Scribner's Sons. Bourke's chief work, *On the Border with Crook,* was also published by Scribner's in 1891. This remains one of the dozen or maybe only half-dozen most illuminating and most readable interpretations of the Southwest of pioneer days yet published. Although about a third of the book deals with General Crook's campaigns against the Sioux, Cheyennes and other horse Indians to the north, the Apaches, the Mexicans, the early-timers, and — always — the natural features of Apache land live through the pages. In 1892 the Bureau of American Ethnology published Bourke's

131

The Medicine Men of the Apache — probably the meatiest thing that has appeared on medicine men of any American tribe.

During nearly a quarter of a century on duty as a soldier in the Southwest, Bourke was absorbing as well as studying the land and its natives. He wrote on "The Folk-Foods of the Rio Grande Valley and of Northern Mexico" and on "Popular Medicine, Customs and Superstitions of the Rio Grande." He contributed ten papers to the *American Anthropologist* and was president of the American Folklore Society when he died. His first book (1884, published by Scribner's) was *The Snake-Dance of the Moquis of Arizona,* the pioneer work on that subject. A student of world folkways, he saw the Apache medicine men not as an isolated species but through the *Arabian Nights* as translated and annotated by Richard F. Burton, through Robert Burton's *Anatomy of Melancholy* and through scores of other works in various languages. The title of his most learned work, *Scatologic Rites of All Nations* (Washington, D.C., 1891), suggests his range and catholicity. He had an urbane perspective, understood relationships and kinships.

Not many scholars of Bourke's latitude and altitude have kept the charm and vividness of his first-person narrative. He was freest as a writer when he could exercise his sense of humor. He belonged in the tradition of humanistic-scientific army officers who, beginning with Lewis and Clark, chartered the Western wilderness not only as to geography but as to flora, fauna, and native tribes. *On the Border with Crook* is dedicated to Francis Parkman "by his admirer and friend." Other scholar-writers whose

132

names are written into the history of the West and who were friends with Bourke include Frank Hamilton Cushing of the Zuñis, Washington Matthews of the Navajos, John Wesley Powell, first understander of the desert West, Jesse Walter Fewkes, George A. Dorsey, and, last of their line, Frederick W. Hodge, who outlived Bourke more than fifty years.

The chief available facts on Bourke's life are in his historical narratives already named and in generous selections from his notebooks edited with biographical sketch and bibliography by Lansing B. Boom and published serially under the title of "Bourke on the Southwest" in the *New Mexico Historical Review* (Vols. VIII-XIII, 1933–1938, and Vol. XIX, 1944).

John Gregory Bourke was born in Philadelphia, June 23, 1846, his father and mother having come over from Ireland as bride and groom about eight years preceding. They were of the upper class, "practical Catholics," with fine linens and liberated minds. Their children — a girl and a boy in addition to John — were brought up in a home of love and books and on the maxim "that a gentleman was ever noble; that his nobility was most surely proved by his quiet, unostentatious kindness to the suffering, and that one of the first Christian duties was to 'visit the sick and bury the dead.' " At the age of eight Bourke was put to studying Greek, Latin and Gaelic.

He ran away from home in 1862 soon after his sixteenth birthday and enlisted in the 15th Pennsylvania Cavalry, serving with it as private throughout the Civil War. He was in various actions. Soon after being mustered out of the service (July, 1865) he was appointed cadet in the

Military Academy at West Point, whence he graduated in June, 1869, the eleventh in a class of thirty-nine. He was later invited back to West Point to teach languages, but declined.

Commissioned second lieutenant, he was assigned at once to the 3rd Cavalry, with which he remained, except when on special duty, the rest of his life. His first post was Fort Craig, on the Rio Grande, from which in January, 1870, he set out for Old Fort Grant in Arizona — "the most forlorn parody upon a military garrison in the most woebegone of military departments." It was only fifty-five desert miles southward — a hard day's ride, two days' march — to Tucson.

Tucson, in which the Shoo-Fly restaurant and the Congress Hall Saloon stood out as prominent institutions, was a mere village, but it was also "the commercial entrepot of Arizona and the remoter Southwest, the Mecca of the dragoon, the Naples of the desert." Not long after Brigadier General George R. Crook arrived in Arizona (1871), Bourke became his aide-de-camp and remained in that intimate position with "my great chief" for many years. On campaigns he acted as adjutant-general and again as engineer officer. A promotion to first lieutenant came in 1876; another to captain in 1882. During all these years he was active in the field most of the time. He had a year off (1881–1882) in which to investigate the manners and customs of the Pueblo, Navajo and Apache Indians — just before taking part in another Apache campaign. Next he took a year's leave of absence to marry and travel in Europe, visiting museums especially. He was with Crook when Geronimo made his final surrender in March, 1886.

In this same year he was "ordered" to Washington to study and to write out his voluminous notes. He remained on this assignment for five years — the most productive of his life so far as writing goes. He was fifteen days short of being fifty years old when he died June 8, 1896.

Only one other writer who penetrated the Southwest during Indian days and "unlocked his word-hoard" on it had gusto, spirit, seeing eyes, hearing ears and power of expression comparable to Bourke's. He was an army officer also (British) but younger and not so ripe: George Frederick Ruxton, who wrote that incomparable book of travels, *Adventures in Mexico and the Rocky Mountains* (1847), and *Life in the Far West* (1848), still quoted by everybody writing on the Mountain Men. These two primary chroniclers had imagination and a sense of style as well as knowledge. Men of action and also of books and thought, both saw violence; but it would never have occurred to either to worship it and thereby to enter into the well-paying kingdom populated by "Westerns."

Bourke knew the right tempo of this land of intense sun, where shaded repose was — and is — supremely valued even in the most violent times. A passage from *On the Border with Crook* and an anecdote from his published notebooks will illustrate not only tempo but humor.

In answer to the inquiry of a stranger in Tucson came this reply:

You want to find the Governor's? Wa'al, podner, jest keep right down this yere street pas the Palace s'loon, till yer gets ter the second manure-pile on yer right, then keep to yer left past the post-office, 'n' yer'll see a dead burro in the middle of th' road, 'n' a mesquite tree 'n yer lef', near a Mexican "tendajon" (small store),

135

'n' jes' beyond that's the Gov.'s outfit. Can't miss it. Look out fur th' dawg down to Munoz's corral, he's a salviated son ov a gun.

Judge Charlie Meyers of Tucson was a terror to evil-doers and an upright, conscientious administrator of justice, although he knew scarcely any law. Being afraid of assassination, he kept in his house after dark. One night in response to a terrible knocking, he roused, raised the little shutter from a hole he had cut in his front door, and demanded to know who is there.

"Me, Jedge."

"And who are you, mine frent?"

"Jedge, I want to give myself up. I've just killed a man."

"Vot you keel him for?"

"He called me a liar en I —"

"Vare you keel him?"

"Down in George Foster's Quartz Rock Gambling Saloon" (a notorious deadfall).

"Very goot, mine frent, dot's all right," said the judge soothingly. "Dot's all right. Go now unt keel unudder von." Then he turned back to bed.

His going-out nature, helped by his linguistic brightness, enabled Bourke to talk with every man in his own language. An Apache scout might be unwilling to give his name to a stranger, but he'd give it to this comrade who was also comrade to the general. Bourke was detailed to use his Spanish in a Pan-American Congress; he laughed with the Mexican servants on the border. He was always wanting to enter the doors of life that he saw ajar. The Apache scouts are having a sweat bath; Bourke must have it with them. Their medicine men are making big medicine; he must sit with them, absorbing lore to go into his pictured pages.

Ethnologists usually write about man or the races of mankind. Bourke wrote about particular men, letting them represent tribes, classes. To him every Apache was an individual. Models of pictorial specification are common in his writings. Take this from *An Apache Campaign*.

All night long the Chiricahuas and the Apache scouts danced together in sign of peace and good-will. The drums were camp-kettles partly filled with water and covered tightly with a well-soaked piece of calico. The drumsticks were willow saplings curved into a hoop at one extremity. The beats recorded one hundred to the minute, and were the same dull, solemn thump which scared Cortez and his beleaguered followers during *la Noche triste*. No Caucasian would refer to it as music; nevertheless, it had a fascination all its own comparable to the whir-r-r of a rattlesnake.

Nobody else has left such luminous sketches of army men at the little forts and camps in Apache days as Bourke. Take his pictures of Captain Russell, an Irishman who had advanced from the ranks, who read science without assimilating it and expressed "moi private opinyun that de whole dam milleetery outfit is going to hell."

A nice little lunch was spread in an adjoining tent, to which any one could repair at pleasure. There was much pleasant converse, story-telling, a little singing and a great deal of drinking. Lieut. Robinson and I being the junior "subs" and also the "staff" of the Battalion, were selected to make the toddies. Neither of us had been trained as a bartender and of course some little preliminary instruction was necessary to enable us to prepare toddies that would pass the inspection of gentlemen of such extended experience in that line as those whom we were serving. We made up in assiduity what we lacked in education, our first effort was pronounced a dead failure; our second was only a shade better. Our third extorted signs of approval. They came rather slowly or reluctantly from the lips of Captain Russell: "I declare to God'l moighty, Mister Robinson, dat's a moighty fine tod-dee; oi tink it wud be a good oidee to put a little more sugar in soak."

You can always judge a man by what he admires. Bourke admired General Crook enormously and must have been distinctly influenced by him. Crook was about the only Indian-fighting general of the West worthy of admiration. Self-righteous O. O. Howard, glory-seeking Custer, Chivington, who was only a colonel but who excelled in pretenses to piety and in brutality, puffed-up Miles, who betrayed good Apaches and Crook both and who lied to the nation — these and some others of their kind seem trivial and base compared to Crook, who was noble and who looms noble in Bourke's noble book.

Books about the West that can be so designated are not numerous, but a high percentage of these that are noble show a strong sympathy for wronged Indians and moral indignation — a virtue that has almost disappeared from the so-called free enterprise newspapers of America — against the wrongers. Crook never relented against the white "vampires" preying on Indians and thriving in times of Indian troubles. He classified most Indian agents as vampires. So did Bourke. All the troubles with the Chiricahua Apaches, Bourke said, could be traced to rotgut whiskey sold them by "worthless white men." Bad as a bad Indian might get, Crook held, "I have never yet seen one so demoralized that he was not an example in honor and nobility compared to the wretches who plunder him of the little our government appropriates for him."

They were both men of strong feelings, decently governed, always on the side of decency and justice. It may be

that his forthright stands and expressed opinions kept
Bourke from rising above the rank of captain during his
third of a century as a soldier. Upon reading, in 1881, that
the tyrannical czar of Russia had been assassinated, Bourke
recorded: "This was a good thing. . . . I hope before
many months to be able to chronicle the assassination of
Bismarck, one of the coldest-blooded and most unprincipled
tyrants who have ever sprung into power." Another diary
record of the same period reads in part:

President Hayes made such an ado about reform in the administration of the government that some people four years ago were deluded
into believing that he was honest in his expressions, but a uniform
duplicity and treachery have convinced the nation that something
besides Appolinaris water at a state dinner or an unctuous outpour-
ing of sanctimonious gab at all times is needed to make a man holy.

Bourke remains very modern.

May 1958

Foreword to
"Recollections of Early Texas,"
by John Holland Jenkins

JOHN HOLLAND JENKINS was thirteen and a half years old when the Alamo fell in 1836 and he became a soldier of the Texas Republic under General Sam Houston. He and his family had been in Texas about eight years. It was not until 1884, when he was past sixty years old, that he began writing down for publication in the Bastrop *Advertiser,* the weekly newspaper of his county, the reminiscences that, as now put into book form, light up for whoever will read the earliest days of early English-speaking Texas.

Jenkins's memories of what happened in his boyhood world are as specific, though not so elaborately detailed, as the childhood and boyhood recollections of W. H. Hudson, Maxim Gorky, Leo Tolstoi, Serghei Aksakoff, and other singular recorders of the far away and long ago in their lives; but Jenkins, so far as his recorded reminiscences go, had no childhood or boyhood. If he recollected any gleams of magic before the light of common day faded them out, he failed to transmit even one of them. He revealed not self but the society of cabin-dwellers, Indian fighters, and buffalo hunters that he belonged to. His reminiscences are the stuff of narrative history concerned with the purely physical but not of the novel that would sound deep into the thoughts, emotions, and sensory experiences of human beings — whether on a frontier of vast vacancies or in a great city outwardly dominated by masses of people and machines.

However that may be, it is something extraordinary to have at this late date a contemporary of one and a third centuries ago speak in fresh accents of those forever vanished times. The cedar logs for the Jenkins cabin, built about forty miles down the Colorado River from where Austin was later to be established as the capital of Texas, were "cut with axes and dragged up with horses." The boards for roof and siding were hand-hewn, from that curious island of pines for which the Bastrop area remains botanically distinguished, and brought by hand and horse to the cabin site and placed without nails. Without mills, the home-raised corn was hand-ground for bread and the high-priced coffee beans were roasted in a pan and then "tied in a piece of buckskin and beaten upon a rock with another rock" to make them release their virtue in boiling water. In the absence of corn, the settlers at times substituted the dried breasts of wild turkeys for bread, eating unsalted venison for meat. There was no money crop and there was virtually no money for these first settlers. A family farm consisted of about ten acres planted by hand in corn, with maybe a dozen rows of cotton, to be cleaned of seeds by hand and home-spun for clothes.

Eli Whitney's body had been moldering in the grave only about three years when the Jenkins family set out from Alabama for Texas. Eli Whitney's cotton gin, invented in 1792, was making planters over the South rich and slaves high and was ginning out the Civil War like the loom of destiny, but such outposts of settlers as the Jenkins community had hardly felt the first breath of industrialization before Josiah Wilbarger was scalped, in 1840.

Texas was still country-living and frontier-minded in 1889, the year that J. W. Wilbarger's *Indian Depredations in Texas* was published and became a household book over the land. Wilbarger made use of the materials now gathered into *Recollections of Early Texas*. He would have been derelict not to have made use of them. The Wilbarger and Jenkins families were old neighbors, friends, and fellow warriors. If *Recollections of Early Texas* had appeared in book form in the 1880's it might have raced *Indian Depredations in Texas* for popularity; the two books are of the same kidney.

They carry one back to the generations of old-timers who considered themselves as having virtually nothing to say unless they could give a firsthand account of an Indian scrape — or of a few killings, preferably involving John Wesley Hardin, Ben Thompson, or some other notability among bad men. The bad men came after the Civil War. Not a single white man killing, unless it has escaped me, occurs in these Jenkins reminiscences of bloodshed and also of white-skinned brutality as naked as any red-skinned. There was hardly another area in Texas that during the process of being "redeemed from the wilderness" suffered so long and so often from Indian molestation, unless it was the Sabinal Canyon country, celebrated by A. J. Sowell in his *Early Settlers and Indian Fighters of Southwest Texas* (1900), and the Parker–Palo Pinto counties area west of Fort Worth.

The man Jenkins made no bones about his preference for Ed Burleson as a leader over Sam Houston. His account of Houston's cursing him is one of the characteristic outright honesties of the book. The feelings between Houston and Burleson were fierce and deep and they were shared by partisans of both leaders. The historical value and interest of this narrative lies to no small extent in the sidelights it throws not only on personalities but on certain vivid episodes — the Runaway Scrape, the Mier Expedition, the Santa Fe Expedition, Texas ranger campaigns, etc.

John Holland Jenkins had little schooling, but a human being's congenital intelligence, memory, and proclivity for observing are not dependent upon schooling. Frequent quotations from classical writers show that Jenkins had read and remembered. He was aware of style in written histories and defined his own purposes in writing. "Little incidents here and there," he observed, "these touches of reality, are necessities in historical narration, just as salt, pepper, and sauce are essential to the right flavoring of soup, roast, and vegetables." Moreover, he felt an inner urge to add to what he entitled "The Treasury of Truth."

Of course, every narrator, whether of fiction or fact, whether writer or talker, knows the effect of detail, for good detail never loses freshness or power to illuminate life. One would have to go no further than the details in this book, cumulative in effect, concerning horses to realize that on the frontiers, as the saying went, a man on foot was no man at all, and that a man on a good horse had the advantage over both nature and enemy.

There was the "Duty Roan," a horse about which tantalizingly little is told. There was Jonathan Burleson —

brother to the great Ed — hemmed up by Indians on a bluff "nearly thirty feet high," but he was riding a good horse, the horse made the tremendous leap, and horse and rider got to safety without a scratch. On one horse raid, Indians stole General Ed Burleson's "celebrated" Scurry, a present to him from one Richard Scurry, manifestly an "American" horse in contradistinction to the low-priced mustang breed. Burleson and eight or ten men took the trail of the horse thieves, but when they caught up with them the general was severely handicapped for want of a horse that could run. One of his party named Spaulding rode the best horse of the lot and when the chase began, across a prairie, Burleson yelled out, "Twenty-five dollars for Scurry, Spaulding!" A little farther on, in a louder voice, Burleson yelled again, "Fifty dollars for Scurry, Spaulding!" And then, as the chase grew hotter, it was, "One hundred dollars for Scurry, Spaulding!" Burleson got Scurry back, but whether Spaulding got the hundred dollars Jenkins does not say.

How the bodies of slain bee hunters were buried in the hollow stump of a bee tree they had cut down, for the discoverers of the bodies had no way of transporting them to a settlement; how the comrades of another man who died far out dug his grave with the "blade bone" of a buffalo and covered him up; how the prairie bottoms were covered with "wild rye," while "sage grass" (little and big bluestem) was high enough for Indians to hide in — these and many other details transport us to the times. Jenkins's prowess as a bee hunter calls up that classic of bee-hunting days, T. B. Tharpe's *The Hive of the Honey-Bee,* in which the hero avers that he could course a bee in the air "a mile away easy." The last sentence in the Jenkins narrative sums up the sympathy for the life with which it is written: "And now, after sixty years of the best hunting, I believe I would ride twenty-five miles [on horseback, of course] to see a fresh bear track."

My people never did believe in voting for a Confederate veteran for public office solely because he was one-armed, one-eyed, half-witted, or possessed of some other defect calculated to influence the majority of voters. When I became acquainted with Johnny (John Holmes III) Jenkins (born March 22, 1940), he was just past fifteen and was doing the research and editorial work that now add much to his great-great-grandfather's *Recollections*. I do not vote for Johnny Jenkins because he became an editor so young but because he has edited so ably. Many a Ph.D. thesis shows less scholarship and less intelligence than Johnny's editorial work and is not nearly so interesting. Some of his notes are for students; some will add to the comprehension of readers in general.

The biographical dictionary at the end of the book is an achievement in usefulness and handiness that might well be adopted by editors of various historical narratives. Like his ancestor, Johnny Jenkins seems to consider it his duty to put down the truth whether it is complimentary or not. As he searches on into the ever-receding Beyond, he will learn that in the realm of thought — perhaps the highest, though not necessarily the most delightful, realm that a historian enters — a great many conclusions based on irrefutable evidence are not patriotic according to politician standards and are not complimentary at all to what Mark Twain dubbed "the damned human race."

145

James Cox and
His "Cattle Industry"*

THE LANDMARKS of a literature seldom graduate to a climax according to chronology. Chaucer died in 1400, Shakespeare in 1616, and in all the intervening centuries, rich though they are in great names, the English language has not achieved another literary peak as lofty as the Chaucerian, much less as the Shakespearian. Among the landmarks distinguishing the development of a literature, historical and otherwise, pertaining to cows, cowmen and cowboys on the grasslands of North America, James Cox's *The Cattle Industry of Texas and Adjacent Territory* stands distinct, though for reasons other than those keeping green the best-known literary names. Furthermore, it is shorter in height than certain landmarks both preceding and succeeding it.

The first landmark remains primary: Joseph G. McCoy's *Historic Sketches of the Cattle Trade,* 1874. Some would account Thomas Pilgrim (who wrote under the name of Arthur Morecamp) the next landmarker, for his *Live Boys: or Charley and Nasho in Texas* (1878) is the first

---

* For all that I have been able to learn about James Cox and his associate S. D. Barnes, I am indebted to the prolonged, far-reaching and most efficient researches of Miss Dorothy A. Brockhoff, reference librarian of Missouri Historical Society, St. Louis.

146

published honest narrative of trail and range — a book designed for boys. Charles A. Siringo's *A Texas Cowboy, or Fifteen Years on the Hurricane Deck of a Spanish Pony* (1885), the first autobiography of an authentic range man, is about as tall as any other landmark in the whole field, despite better-written and otherwise better books dealing with range life. Cox's *Cattle Industry* (1895) is the next landmark. Then in rapid succession come two novels by Owen Wister and Andy Adams, *The Virginian* (1902) and *The Log of a Cowboy* (1903), followed by *Prose and Poetry of the Live Stock Industry of the United States* (1905). We need not specify on more recent landmarks.

Like the Cox volume, *Prose and Poetry* is a combination of history and biographical sketches, but it is better written and more richly illustrated throughout; the sketches are far more interesting because they are generally far more concrete in detail, and the history conveys more knowledge and a juster sense of values, coming from a wider perspective. The Cox volume was, in fact, designed primarily as a mug book, though history is the gainer through information conveyed in numerous mug sketches; others are little more than blurbs. The Cox volume contains 449 biographical sketches concentrated into 393 pages of text, averaging less than a page each. *Prose and Poetry* has only 44 biographical sketches, occupying about 222 pages, averaging five pages each, scattered in a haphazard way through 757 pages of text — say 535 pages of history. Cox has only 293 pages left for history, and 60 pages of this are given over to writeups, advertising in nature, of railroads and livestock commission firms.

147

According to doubtful tradition, the Cox volume sold upon publication for $25. My conjecture is that the book never went on the general market, was not offered to bookstores but only to individuals and businesses represented in it, and even then was not bought by all the "mugs" included in its pages. Years ago H. M. Sender of Kansas City, dealer in Western Americana, procured, one by one, a considerable number of the books from descendants of biographized cowmen that he traced down. It must have cost any subject an additional price to have his picture in the book. Though quoted on range history, Dudley H. Snyder and A. S. Mercer (author of *Banditti of the Plains*), names still well remembered, are omitted from the biographical record. J. M. Mathis is well represented, but his partners Tom Coleman and C. W. Fulton, still big names, of the Coleman, Mathis and Fulton Pasture Company are omitted. Ike Pryor, a bigshot during and after trail-driving days, was always in heat for publicity, but he is left out of this book, along with George West, Cyrus B. Lucas and other notabilities. Presumably some of them wouldn't pay, and some didn't get a chance to pay.

Henry R. Wagner once asserted — perhaps in a perverse mood — that no really good book becomes rare in the sense that it can't be bought for a reasonable price in some edition, and that no "rare" book is good. Collectors with money make certain books rare, the rareness depending upon three qualities of conditions: (1) paucity of copies; (2) the sheeplike nature of many collectors in disregarding intrinsic merit and in being hell-bent on owning something that few others can own; (3) least of all, the inherent values, human and humanistic, of a book. How many copies of Cox's *Cattle Industry* were printed cannot be ascertained. Old records of the printing company were destroyed when it moved into a new building several decades ago, and a search through newspapers and farm and ranch magazines of 1894 and 1895 has yielded no mention of the book. Ponderous and bound in leather, it was expensive to manufacture even 65 years ago. There would have been slight reason for manufacturing more than six or seven hundred copies. They simply do not show up nowadays, even at $500 a copy.

Going on what H. M. Sender told him orally around 1935, Wright Howes set down in *U.S.-iana* (1954) this sentence respecting the Cox: "Nearly the entire edition burned in warehouse before copies circulated." I think that the people who ordered books got them. I know that my uncle Jim (J. M.) Dobie, whose sketch, banally composed, appears in the book, got his copy; I traded a pair of ten-dollar store-bought boots, which did not fit, for it to his brother Neville, another dear uncle, in 1928. Alas for the fallibility of human memory — my own especially! I wrote friend Sender for a more detailed statement and now quote from his reply of October 5, 1959:

I have forgotten the date, but it was, I think, between 20 or 25 years ago, that I called upon the Woodward & Tiernan Printing Company in St. Louis, Missouri, publishers of Cox's *Cattle Industry of Texas*. At the time they had one remaining copy on hand, and I purchased it.

They told me that they had had an old warehouse in which they stored various things, including a lot of books out of print, and, they thought, of no value. They needed more space and decided to wreck the old warehouse and build a new building on the ground. They either burned or had hauled away several lots of books. Among the discards, so they said, were about 35 or 40 copies of the Cox "Cattle Book." I never inquired how many were printed or how much they sold for.

Cox was a practiced hand with mug and chamber-of-commerce booster books. *Notable St. Louisans in 1900: A Portrait Gallery of Men Whose Energy and Ability Have Contributed Largely Towards Making St. Louis the Commercial and Financial Metropolis of the West, Southwest and South,* edited by James Cox, and published — or, more properly, printed — in St. Louis in 1900, was pure mug. Writing on "A Century of Missouri Literature" (in the *Missouri Historical Review* for October, 1920) Alexander Nicolas De Menil characterizes the Cox titles as "mere compilations made to order for subscription companies or advertising firms." They were mostly printed in St. Louis, where during the last ten years or so of his life Cox was secretary of the Louisiana Purchase Exposition Company, secretary of the Bureau of Information for St. Louis Autumnal Festivities Association, secetary of the Business Men's League, etc. His *St. Louis Through a Camera* (1892) and *Old and New St. Louis* (1894) were evidently for the tourist trade. *Our Own Country* (1894) and *My Native Land* (1895) seem to have been intended for wider audiences, though they have that come-hither, booster quality. They are composed of journalistic sketches; while not histories, they are better written than those textbooks of dullness and stupidities palmed off on the public schools of America by Ph.D.'s from Education — spelled with a capital E — departments.

150

If *The Cattle Industry* were not distinctly more than a mug book, it would not be republished now — with this introduction. Many, probably the majority, of the biographical sketches contain all the available facts on certain range men. Interesting details of the best sketches were utilized by the biographers of *Prose and Poetry of the Cattle Industry*. Cox avowedly did not write them but manifestly did write the historical chapters. The essay on "The Cowboy, as He Was, and Is, and Is Supposed to Have Been" is an extension of a chapter in Cox's *My Native Land,* published also in 1895. As far as it goes, this essay seems to me as good as the characterizations found in expositions on the cowboy by Emerson Hough and Philip Ashton Rollins. To be sure, Cox's cowboy is unsexed and orthodoxly Victorian, as he remained in virtually all writing touching him between McCoy's *Historic Sketches of the Cattle Trade* (1874) and rollicky *We Pointed Them North* as told by Teddy Blue Abbott to Helena Huntington Smith (1939); Patrick Tucker's *Riding the High Country* (1933) had suggested considerable and Walker D. Wyman's *Nothing but Prairie and Sky* (1954) carried the flag several notches higher out of the Valley of Eunuchal Pretense.

Disillusioned, frenetical, headlong Joseph G. McCoy believed in calling a spade a spade, though he was restrained by the Kansas blend of religion and aesthetics that denatured a bull painted in full possession of his virility across the front of the Bull's Head Saloon in Abilene. Just the same, McCoy's picture of a Texas cowboy fresh off the trail at a whorehouse dance in a cowtown was too strong for succeeding mythmakers on the type: ". . . the front of his sombrero lifted at an angle of fully forty-five degrees; his huge spurs jingling at every step or motion; his revolvers flapping up and down like a retreating sheep's tail; his eyes lit up with excitement, liquor and lust." Of course, the cowboy tamed down considerably between 1867, when McCoy met him, and 1895, but his eyes still "lit up."

When it came to portraying a cowman, McCoy belonged more to the outspoken seventeenth century than to the covering-up age in which we still live. An extract from his sketch on Abel Head (better known as Shanghai) Pierce will illustrate:

In a few years [on his Rancho Grande in Texas] he so increased his stock of cattle that in the year 1871 he branded fifteen thousand eight hundred head of calves and "mavvericks." Indeed it was ominously hinted that Pierce's New England energy was too great for his competitors and other neighboring ranchers, and that they became jealous of his success, and did not stop at calling him names more expressive than complimentary; but inaugurated a semi-belligerent state of affairs, in which both parties took an active part. From time to time various cow-boys on both sides were missed, but afterward found dead with their boots on. Finally this state of affairs began to take the dimensions of a small war; but upon one fine morning seven or eight Mexican and other cow-boys belonging to the ranks of Pierce's mortal enemies, were seen hanging to the limbs of a dead tree as human fruit. Pierce says: "Had that tree been green and alive, he don't know how much larger crop it would have borne." That vexatious and ever meddling institution called a grand jury, was more officious about this and other similar occurrences than was comfortable or pleasing to Pierce, so he sold out his interest in the fine large stock he had become part owner of, for a snug sum of money, and went into Kansas to trade in cattle; where he has since occupied his attention and capital in various large transactions in live stock. Of late every one who visits the western cattle market

sees or hears of "Shanghai Pierce." And if they ever get within can-
non shot of where he is, they hear his ear-splitting voice more pierc-
ing than a locomotive whistle — more noisy than a steam calliope. It
is idle to try to dispute or debate with him, for he will overwhelm
you with indescribable noise, however little sense it may convey. . . .
He is in the fullest sense a self-made man, which is not to be con-
strued as relieving the Creator of great responsibility. There are few
cattle dealers better calculated for, or more determined on, taking
care of themselves than A. H. Pierce.

The nearest the Pierce sketch in Cox comes to such
realism is:

In January of 1871 Mr. Pierce's wife died, and as he had been having sundry troubles and was not perfectly in accord with the State
Administration in matters of politics and religion [presumably respecting mavericks and cowhides], he sold out his cattle interests for
$100,000 in gold and went to Kansas City to enjoy a little well-
earned rest and the pleasures of society.

Prose and Poetry leaves "Old Shang" out. The biography (1953) by Chris Emmett leaves out Shanghai's
notorious balls. Some writers say what they want to say in
fiction, but in biography the roosters are mostly capons.

The printed sources that Cox had to draw on for his
"historical record" were limited as compared with what is
now available. He made use of most of the best then available, though he seems to have been unaware of Siringo's
autobiography and of Nimmo's excellent *The Range and
Ranch Cattle Traffic in the Western States and Territories,*
a government publication of 1885. He himself had been at
the noted convention of cowmen in St. Louis in 1884. He
had sought out range men for their experiences. He did not

let what he did not know bother him a great deal. He was a skilled reporter and had the power to blend his knowledge into a readable narrative. He followed Herodotus and Macaulay in the idea that history should be readable — an idea bludgeoned into bog by the Ph.D.ism of Teutonic turgidity. Reminiscences such as *Cowboy Life in Texas* by W. S. James — still superior to everything else written by Will James, Cox observed — "do more to depict the condition of the cattle industry at the time of the war [over barbed wire] than any sternly written record could possibly do."

The ability to quote Dickens helped Cox in selecting quotations from *Frank Leslie's Magazine* and the *Texas Stockman and Farmer*. He was better informed on the nature of range cattle, as his treatment of stampedes illustrates, than any scriptwriter Hollywood has ever utilized to picture cattle in a herd, on the trail, or anywhere else. He had an ear for picturesque speech, but he did not throw off on economic statistics or on such subjects as the evolution of hat, boots, saddle and other ranch country equipment. He wrote before the fever tick was discovered to be the cause of what was called "Texas," "Spanish," "Southern" fever in cattle. His chapter on the subject is now interesting in the way that a history of blood-letting by doctors is interesting. Some of the cowman testimony quoted on the "fever" illustrates the abiding truth that a greed-dominated man recognizes in others no other motive than greed.

James Cox must have been responsible for picking S. [Sylvester] D. Barnes as "editor of a majority of the biographies" in his cattle book (page 247), but information on Barnes has eluded extensive searchings. In 1894 he for a few months edited *Outdoor Sports and American Angler,* a semimonthly magazine printed in St. Louis, until another man took it over and moved it to New York. Thenceforth Barnes disappears from the record. Who the "representatives" were that "traveled through Texas gathering" data for the biographical sketches — and also, no doubt, names on dotted lines — is unknown to me.

The facts on Cox himself are hard to pin down. A biographical sketch, for which he evidently furnished the data, in Hyde and Conard's *Encyclopedia of the History of St. Louis* (1899) seems more trustworthy than newspaper obituaries, which are contradictory on some points.

James Cox was born in Horncastle, Lincolnshire, England, January, 1851. He went to a "public school" — the British term for what in the United States is called a private school. That he could have graduated from Oxford, "with honors in history and jurisprudence" — as recorded in several St. Louis publications — without leaving his name on record at Oxford seems incredible. It does not appear in Foster's carefully compiled *Alumni Oxonienses;* the head clerk of Oxford University Registry avers in a letter of 1959 that no record of him exists there.

Again, if James Cox became, as repeatedly reported in St. Louis print, "reporter and field correspondent" for *The Times* of London, covering the bombardment of Alexandria (1882) and the Soudan War (1884–1885), there should be some record of him, it would seem, in the office of that great newspaper. Miss Dorothy A. Brockhoff, reference librarian of the Missouri Historical Society in St. Louis, asked Mr. W. A. Hayward of the Monsanto

155

Chemical Company in London to investigate. The librarian of *The Times* made search and reported to him that the newspaper's records contain nothing on James Cox as an employee or otherwise.

The St. Louis *Encyclopedia* lists among Cox's writings *A Romance of Medway*, "published in 1875, his first more ambitious effort," and *From Dongola to Khartoum*, "written in 1885." Neither of these titles is in the British Museum, the Bodleian Library, the Library of Congress or any other listed repository of books.

Anyhow, having married Annie Jackson, Cox and his bride came to America and straightway settled in St. Louis, where he got a job reporting on the *Globe-Democrat*. By 1889, having meanwhile tried weekly newspapering in Kansas, he was assistant managing editor. He resigned to work on an evening paper, soon becoming managing editor of the *Star-Sayings*.

In 1891 he began his career as what would now be called public relations agent. The magazine articles that he turned out for *Frank Leslie's Popular Monthly, Lippincott's* and other magazines were almost altogether about St. Louis. "Sanitary Science in the West," which appeared in *The New England Magazine* (May, 1892), merely "booms" the St. Louis water system.

Cox belonged to the Writers Club of St. Louis, attended its social-literary meetings frequently and in 1892 read at least two papers before it. One of them, "The Press of Two Continents," reproduced in *The Spectator* (St. Louis), still makes fair reading — urbane, ironic, sophisticated, superficial.

156

William Marion Reedy, editor and owner of the once famed *Mirror,* published in St. Louis, took a malicious pleasure in throwing *banderillas* into the literary hide of "Mr. James Falsetto Cox," "grass widow of the Writers Club," though when Cox died he characterized him as "indefatigable in his willingness to do his best" and as "affability itself." According to one account, Cox lost his voice in the Soudan campaign; according to another, told by him, he lost it sprinting for five miles near Windsor Castle to see some notability he had to report on. The titles of *Our Own Country* and *My Native Land* suggest that Cox did not want to be taken for an outsider. His English accent — the accent of a cultivated gentleman — must have been burdensome to him at times.

James Cox died on December 2, 1901 — not in 1902 as has been published on Library of Congress catalogue cards and elsewhere. He was buried in the Bellefontaine Cemetery of St. Louis, to which his wife followed in 1904. Their adopted son, Raymond Jackson Cox, born in 1891, was already with her family in England. According to her will, he was to be sent to Oxford should he so desire. No record indicates that he had such a desire, but he was well provided for in money and other property, Cox himself having left his wife "a big estate"— the inventory entered in the probate court nominating numerous city lots, 24 rent flats, "a number of acres in Aransas County, Texas," and $10,058 in the bank. When his wife died, her property, according to inventory, was bringing in towards $10,000 per year.

"They are all gone now," bereft Nora in Synge's *Riders to the Sea* says. *Historical and Biographical Record of the*

157

Cattle Industry and the Cattlemen of Texas and Adjacent Territory is the only thing left from all the Cox striving. As things go, it is monument enough for a man of his stature.

Helen Hunt Jackson
and "Ramona"

THE FACTS — the outside facts, which are the only documentable facts about any life — outlining the career of Helen Hunt Jackson are not nearly so romantic as the romance on which her fame rests. They are to be found, thoroughly sifted and footnoted, in the biography *Helen Hunt Jackson,* by Ruth Odell, to which scholarly work I express my debt.

Helen Maria Fiske was born in Amherst, Massachusetts, October 15, 1830. Both her parents were of old, respectable, God-fearing New England families. Her father, Nathan Welby Fiske, had been educated in theology, but his love of the classics was almost as fierce as his piety. He was professor in languages and rhetoric at Amherst College. His wife, born Deborah Waterman Vinal, had a strong mind and strong religious feelings. She taught little Helen to pray that her brandy-drinking grandfather "become pious."

Helen was a headstrong child. At five, reading the *Youth's Companion* was her delight. At eleven she was sent off to a private school in Hadley, Massachusetts. She was tractable enough but refused to go to Sunday school until her mother wrote that she wished her to go. In one

159

of many letters to her daughter, Deborah Fiske expressed the hope that God had "opened" Helen's eyes to see "the evil of having sinned against Him without any regret so many years." Every proper New Englander at that time knew he or she had been conceived in sin and lived in sin, although the nature of unintended sin might not be clear to a little girl — or even to a big man.

Her mother died before Helen was fourteen years old. Her father died three years later. Meantime, her education went on. She grew up knowing scholars and writers. In 1852 at the age of twenty-two she married Lieutenant Edward B. Hunt. A scientist, he was in the Coast Survey Department and had to travel a great deal, but they made their home in Washington. Here Helen Hunt came to know more of the "right people." During the Civil War, Lieutenant Hunt was promoted to major. They had two children, but both died in infancy. Major Hunt died late in 1863.

Helen's first contributions were signed "Marah." She did not like the name Helen Hunt on account of its alliterative connotations. For a while she used "H.H."; then she gave those initials up for "Rip Van Winkle," "Saxe Holm," and the complete anonymity of "No Name." Her chief guide and counsel was Colonel Thomas Wentworth Higginson, a pillar of the Boston and Concord Brahmins. She wrote for the *New York Independent,* for the *Nation, Riverside Magazine, St. Nicholas,* and then in time for the *Century Magazine* and the *Atlantic Monthly.* She dallied with the theory of evolution, was praised by Emerson, but nothing inside herself burned to get out. In 1874, after trips west for copy, she married William Sharpless Jackson, of Colorado Springs, Colorado. Railroad capitalist, banker, and civilized gentleman, he was a famous host for his wife's friends as well as for his own. Her home for the remainder of her life was in Colorado Springs. She traveled a great deal, however — to Europe as well as to the East — and one wonders how she managed to have the head of her bed always turned to the north in hotels, on sleeping cars, and elsewhere. She claimed she could not sleep unless her head was pointed north. Maybe she didn't have to sleep on a bed.

In 1879 she was in Boston to help celebrate Oliver Wendell Holmes's seventieth birthday. While there, she heard Standing Bear and Bright Eyes lecture on the wrongs of the Ponca Indians. Standing Bear spoke with dignity and indignation, and Bright Eyes interpreted his eloquence with wonderful facility. Helen Hunt Jackson was fired with sympathy for the Poncas and then for other Indians. She burned with indignation against the corrupt "Indian Ring." Thenceforward she had to say something. In the *New York Tribune* and elsewhere she castigated Secretary of the Interior Carl Schurz. She spent months doing research in the Astor Library in New York City, fortifying herself on facts. The result was *A Century of Dishonor*.

This book, which appeared in 1881, and *Ramona*, 1884, were the only two of her works that Helen Hunt Jackson signed her full name to. *A Century of Dishonor* was bound in blood-red cloth on which was stamped a quotation from Benjamin Franklin: "Look upon your hands! They are stained with the blood of your relations." She sent a copy of the book to every member of Congress. Despite its

161

earnestness — maybe because of too much earnestness along with too little skill in writing — it is dull.

Soon after its publication, she came to southern California, gathering information for a series of articles on the missions and Indians of the region for *Century Magazine*. From people and the land itself, over which she was horse-drawn, she acquired the background for *Ramona*. She was committed to what is called romance; she was also committed to the cause of California Indians. She proposed that *Ramona* do for them what *Uncle Tom's Cabin* had done for the Negroes. She was a dedicated woman — more dedicated to a cause than to craftsmanship.

On August 8, 1885, four days before she died, she wrote Grover Cleveland, President of the United States, as follows:

From my deathbed I send you message of heartfelt thanks for what you've already done for the Indians. I ask you to read my *Century of Dishonor*. I am dying happier for the belief I have that it is your hand that is destined to strike the first steady blow toward lifting this burden of infamy from our country and righting the wrongs of the Indian race.

Nobody can question the integrity of Helen Hunt Jackson's motives, but history may ask how far she was right in her pictures of mission Indians and of the missions and missionaries. Maybe she was as right as Harriet Beecher Stowe was in her picture of the Negroes. Agnes Repplier once said that the abolition of any institution capable of producing such paragons of virtue as Uncle Tom could have been an error in judgment. *Uncle Tom's Cabin*, just the same, had a powerful effect in rousing sentiment against slavery. *Ramona* had no such effect in arousing sentiment for the rights, or even the betterment, of Indians. Its main effect was to romanticize the mission period of California history and those mission relics left for tourist visitation on the California landscape.

According to *Ramona,* the missions meant not only salvation for Indian souls but an idyllic physical existence, the padres standing as their sole protection against the materialistic world. As a matter of fact, though not according to chamber-of-commerce legend, Spanish missions always worked hand in hand with the military. The missions in California were kept populated by military capture of Indians who wanted to remain wild and free. The Spanish word for a mission Indian was *Indio reducido* — a reduced Indian. He was reduced from freedom.

The mission fathers kept vital statistics, on births, deaths, marriages, etc., conscientiously. Primary among the sources where those statistics are now to be consulted are the scholarly studies by Dr. S. F. Cook, of the University of California. His studies are widely scattered in learned journals but have been digested into Carey McWilliams's excellent *Southern California Country.* From 1769 to 1833, the California mission records list 29,100 Indian births and 62,600 Indian deaths. During the same period of mission rule, according to figures assembled by Dr. Cook, some of them in this instance necessarily estimates, the Indian population of California declined from 130,000 in 1769 to 83,000 in 1832.

When the missions were secularized in 1834 — secularized according to the original Spanish laws of colonization — the mission neophytes passed without abruptness into a

163

state of peonage. During the next decade and more, until the United States took formal possession of California in 1848, the dons were at their climax.

American rule in California resulted in three statutes vitally affecting the Indians. One statute, not repealed until 1872, provided that no Indian could testify in court. Another provided that Indians might be declared vagrants upon the petition of a white person; a third permitted the apprenticing — actually peonizing — of Indian children with the "consent" of their parents. Most of the apprentices went to the ranchero dons.

While all Spanish and Mexican land grants that could be proven legal were confirmed by the United States government, not many of the dons could adjust themselves to the greedy, pushing ways of English-speaking citizens who rushed into California following the discovery of gold. The dons had crossbred prolifically enough with Indian women, but they had looked down their noses at all *mestizos* — the Mexicans. Now the displaced dons had to coalesce with the Mexicans in order to hold even a part of their own against the English-speakers.

At the very time Helen Hunt Jackson was espousing the cause of the descendants of the mission Indians, California promoters decided that a great and paying attraction for tourists and other romance-seekers would be the dons and the missions. As a result of commercial ballyhoo, *Ramona,* instead of becoming the battle hymn for the more and more displaced and more and more reduced Indians that Helen Hunt Jackson had hoped for, became, contrary to its contents, a signal mountain of romance for the "days of the Dons" and for the missions. Well into the twentieth century, until about the time of World War II, as many places in southern California claimed to be the authentic habitation, marriage ground, or something else for the original of Ramona as houses in another part of the United States claimed to be where George Washington slept. Those office-complexioned, pot-bellied members of the Rotary Club who ride Palomino horses in the Rose Parade at Pasadena each wintry spring are about as authentic in representing Spanish dons as *Ramona* is in historical values on Spanish missions and the Indian life at them.

Yet *Ramona* is authentic. No more authentic chapter exists in the great American determination to get away from reality than the *Ramona* legend. It is entirely fitting that politicians most determined to take Formosa for China — equivalent to taking Catalina Island for California — during the 1950's should come from the land of the dons and of *Ramona.*

Of course, Ramona can still be read with interest as a story, though some readers brought up on American fiction from the time of Frances Newman's *The Hard-Boiled Virgin* until *The Naked and the Dead, Lolita,* and other contemporary novels might find some of the sobbing and praying in *Ramona* tedious. Offsetting sentimentality are swiftness of action and suspense. The suspense probably reaches its climax while Ramona is waiting for Allesandro to come and deliver her from the tyranny of a don's widow. (*Alessandro* is grand opera Italian, *Alejandro* being the Spanish-Mexican spelling.)

The business of all workers at the hacienda sticking their heads out in the morning and singing a prayer is idealization. Haciendas were not run that way. On the other hand, the pictures of sheep shearing and of the goings-on at Hartsel's Tavern are earthily realistic. Accounts of eviction of the Indians from their native grounds are based on firsthand observations and are hardly overdrawn. The cupidity of Americans in taking the land from the aborigines of America can hardly be overdrawn. This cupidity, linked sometimes with thrifty piety and sometimes with ostentatious religiosity, was at the basis of the often expressed progressive American philosophy toward Indians in general: "The only good Indian is a dead Indian." The zeal for goodness converted many Indians trying to hold their lands against the zealots.

People have done a great many things to southern California while gardening, Hollywooding, and Disneylanding it. They have changed the climate of the inhabited parts of it as people have not been able to change the climate anywhere else on earth. As octopus-sprawling Los Angeles comes more and more to be southern California, the smog that people have created over it refuses most stubbornly to be uncreated. John Steinbeck belongs north of southern California. His *Grapes of Wrath,* nevertheless, is southern and is the strangest fruit that California, either north or south, has produced. It is strange because in its Okie realism it is utterly unlike the standard literary fruit of California.

The things that people have done to southern California are minor compared to what southern California has done to most people who have gone there. Exceptions may be found in factories and in the California Institute of Technology, but in fiction as well as in come-hither advertise-

ments, California has been the place of all places where
Formosa is China.

Take Abbot Kinney. Originally of New Jersey, he was
no more southern California in origin, education, and experience than Helen Hunt Jackson was. He was made Indian commissioner with her. "A Report on the Condition
and Needs of the Mission Indians of California, made by
special agents Helen Hunt Jackson and Abbot Kinney, to
the Commissioner of Indian Affairs," dated July, 1883,
has appeared as an appendix in all copies of *A Century of
Dishonor* published since 1885. Kinney established Venice,
now within the corporate limits of Los Angeles. Here he
dug canals and imported gondolas and gondoliers from
Italy to move on the canal waters. A summary on him by
Franklin D. Walker in *A Literary History of Southern
California,* a work sometimes ironic and all the time divert-
ing and enlightening, is too illuminating on the presmog
aura not to quote:

Abbot Kinney has been described as "a student of law and medicine, commission merchant, botanical expert, cigarette manufacturer,
and member of the United States Geological Survey." Ever since
Kinney had inherited half of the Sweet Caporal fortune before he
was thirty, the blue-eyed, sorrel-thatched adventurer had been looking for interesting things to do. For a while he roamed in Africa
and Asia; then, in 1880, he settled near Pasadena, on the ranch
which he named Kinneyloa — "Kinney" for himself and "loa" for
the Hawaiian word for hill. After touring the Indian country with
Mrs. Jackson, he became an enthusiast for marriage, and, finding a
mate — whom he called another Helen Hunt Jackson — in the
daughter of a San Francisco judge, proceeded to illustrate the theories of "creative reproduction," which he had put forth in his *Tasks
by Twilight,* by fathering nine children. In the meantime and in be-

tween he helped to develop Yosemite as a national park, aided in securing the local enactment of the Australian ballot law, furthered the establishment of federal forest reserves, pioneered in the use of the eucalyptus tree in California, helped to found public libraries at Pasadena and Venice, and edited and published a local agricultural journal entitled *Los Angeles Saturday Post; Fruit, Forest, and Farm* (1900–1906).

Three-quarters of a century after the author of *Ramona* died her chief work lives on, not only in print but in the minds and emotions of people who call for the book in libraries, buy it in stores, read it, and are moved by it. At least three motion picture versions of it have been produced. A Ramona pageant, "California's Greatest Outdoor Play," produced by the Hemet Chamber of Commerce, still brings each year devotees of the story of the Indian lovers — also others — to an amphitheater in the San Jacinto Valley.

It is something to believe steadfastly and disinterestedly in anything good for any part of mankind. It is something to be capable of and to express deep moral indignation. This age of executive ambition and of religiosity-pays-in-business has allowed the fires of moral indignation to sink almost into the ashes. Helen Hunt Jackson's outcries of moral indignation against America's shifty and cruel treatment of Indians still lift human spirits — even though comparatively few people are moved to lift hands against ambitious patriots still trying to get hold of Indian property. The noblest of all Indian fighters of the U.S. Army was General George Crook. The noblest of all books about these fighters is Captain John G. Bourke's *On the Border with Crook*. Both Crook and Bourke burned with indignation against the American leeches responsible for Indian outbreaks. Helen Hunt Jackson belongs in the not-numerous company ennobled by General Crook and Captain Bourke. Her passion against wrong and for right will make her book live a long, long while yet. Called a historical novel, now it belongs to history.

Spring 1959

Introduction to
"Home on the Double Bayou,"
by Ralph Semmes Jackson

LAND HAS BEEN PERSONAL to me from the time I began having feelings. Certain live oaks, certain patches of grass, certain bends in Ramirenia Creek, certain mustang grapevines draping trees along the bank, certain hills on the ranch where I was born and reared remain more vivid to me and are more a part of me than numbers of people I knew while I was putting down roots into that plot of earth. One time when I came home (several years after the family had moved from the ranch to Beeville) and a few hours later was setting out for the ranch, my mother said, "Why, Son, you think more of the ranch than of your own people." Whatever in the land pulled me, it was not property values. They were meager anyhow.

But after my mother died in 1948 and the ranch was inherited by six brothers and sisters, it had to become property. My sister Fannie and I were executors. In 1951 we sold it to Ralph Jackson and five other men associated with him. He was the leader. From the minute I looked at his features of cultivated intelligence and heard his gentle voice, I was satisfied with the inevitable transference of deeds to the land. I had strong feelings on who should possess the deeds and would not have transferred them at any price to a certain individual who came trying to buy.

Ralph Jackson's reminiscences are not so personal to me as the ranch in Live Oak County that he also is coming to cherish, but they are more than passingly personal. Something over a year ago he paid me a brief visit and hesitatingly left a manuscript to read, and as I understood, to keep. He had made several copies of it. He gave me to understand that what he had written of boyhood experiences on the Jackson ranch in Chambers County and of his people there was for his children and for their children to come so that they might better value their human inheritance. He judged that I might find something of interest in the narrative. I read it almost immediately, charmed with the pictures of people and animals, with a boy's experiences, and, above all, with the atmosphere of serenity and simple sincerity. I telephoned my friend Frank Wardlaw, director of the University of Texas Press, and told him that I had the makings of a book he was going to publish. Ralph Jackson had no more expected this than he had expected to be appointed dictator of the Dominican "Republic." Yet he was by no means displeased when the press proposed an expansion of the reminiscences, along with certain rearrangements of subject matter, into a book. Galley proofs have given me those feelings of refreshment that the preliminary sketches gave.

In a way the chronicle parallels the ancient trunks up in the attic of the JHK ranch house "stuffed with three generations" of discarded clothes and other keepsakes. The recollections of three generations — Grandpa James Jackson, founder of the ranch, being the most amply revealed

171

character of the book — enforce a definition I once tried to make of a home. Ideally, I said, a home is a residing place enriched by the accretions of human living over several generations, each inheriting something of the ways and experiences of forebears and each weaving its own life into a texture of tradition. This conception, of course, implies more permanence in houses and more permanence in the occupancy of them than the machine-driven ways of American life have come to permit. The sellers, who make more noise than everybody else put together, could not dictate their form of "progress" if large numbers of families remained planted, accommodating themselves to seasons and shadows rather than to annual new models. While exuding the aroma of tradition, *Home on the Double Bayou* is not at all a traditional book. It illustrates the fact that carrying on a good tradition requires creative energy and is not accomplished merely through passive inheritance.

The writer is a part of the parcel of land about which he writes, and reading of it, I find the parcel of land to which I belong stirring within me, though my land is long on drouths and thorns, while his is lush from rain, bounded by water, and so lacking in rocks that a visit to shipping pens eighteen miles away meant to a boy a supply of pebbles from railroad ballast to shoot in a niggershooter. Had this sensitive recollector of boyhood sensations been writing a ranch book in traditional style, he would have emphasized such things as the White Ranch — site of the shipping pens — from which on the very day of the battle of San Jacinto a herd of beeves was being trailed to the New Orleans market. More vivid to me than any other bovine critter on the Jackson ranch is a goose-hunting steer who collaborated with his shotgun-armed owner; yet a description of more than two thousand head of prairie cattle piling up against a barbed-wire fence and freezing to death in attempts to reach shelter against a wet norther is rangy enough.

Home on the Double Bayou is more akin to W. H. Hudson's *Far Away and Long Ago* than to the stream of books — scores of them vapid and false — purporting to give ranch experiences. The kinship is not literary; there is no evidence that Ralph Jackson has read *Far Away and Long Ago*. The kinship is in pictures of reality fresh out of boyhood, untarnished by "the world's slow stain." A parallel to a character who came to the Hudson *estancia* on the pampas is "The Stranger," an Englishman, who one day drove up to Grandpa Jackson's ranch in his buggy and stayed three years without telling his name. He tutored several of the eleven children, read aloud to the family classical books "out of the depth of his trunk," transmitted to one boy almost totally blind the lifetime solace of drawing beautiful music from a violin, and then one morning, after remarking that he must leave, drove away. The kinship comes to me in minute accounts of animal life, always specific, never generalized, as exemplified by the clouds and heaps of mosquitoes, at certain times, in certain places. It lies in the maintenance from the first paragraph to the last of a quiet tempo of life. One sentence from the chapter entitled "Our Railroad" will illustrate the tempo: "In the middle of the morning and afternoon the engineer would pull the train to a creaking halt opposite some lonely ranch house and proceed to take the entire train crew over to it for a leisurely cup of coffee

173

and a neighborly visit." Ralph Jackson is still a comparatively young man, but he also has written of far away and long ago when a boy would spend hours sprawled on the ground circumventing a tumblebug but finally letting him move on with his marble-sized riches. That boy, walking away from the tumblebug, was joyfully unaware of having through "a wise passiveness" seeped up from the earth something that would to him be a solace and restorer in all the years to come. It is not often that one finds in a modern book the Ralph Jackson blend of spiritual and of good earth gladness.

In Austin, Texas
Where "the leafy month" is April
1961

A Summary Introduction
to Frederic Remington

FREDERIC REMINGTON WORKED for only about twenty-five years. During the half-century that has raced by since he died just past his forty-eighth birthday — still in the Horse Age — his fame as depictor of the Old West has not perceptibly diminished. Yet no adequate life of him has been published. The one considerable piece of writing on his life and work worthy of respect by people entitled to an opinion is the chapter "Remington in Kansas" (pages 194–211, plus a wealth of notes, pages 355–363) in *Artists and Illustrators of the Old West,* 1850–1900, by the late Robert Taft, of the University of Kansas, published by Charles Scribner's Sons, New York, 1953. The present essay owes far more to this noble work of vast knowledge, all ordered and evaluated, and of quiet power than to all other sources.

Frederic Remington, Artist of the Old West, by Harold McCracken, 1947, contains a useful bibliography of Remington's writings, books illustrated by him, appearances in periodicals, and his bronzes.

Remington's own writings — all illustrated — are the best sources for facts and understanding about him, but many of them in magazines antedating his death — in-

175

cluding the autobiographical sketch in *Collier's Weekly* (New York, March 18, 1905)— are available in only a few libraries.

The most knowledgeable person alive on Remington is probably Miss Helen L. Card, proprietor of the Latendorf Bookshop (containing more art than books), 714 Madison Avenue, New York. She does not publish enough, but her two pamphlets, privately printed at Woonsocket, Rhode Island, 1946, on *A Collector's Remington* (I. "Notes on Him; Books Illustrated by Him; and Books Which Gossip About Him." II. "The Story of His Bronzes, with a Complete Descriptive List") contain as much concentrated protein as wheat germ.

Frederic Sackrider Remington was born of parents strong of body and character in Canton, New York, October 1, 1861. His father owned and edited the local newspaper but left it to fight for the Union. Frederic, an only child, early learned to swim, fish, and play Indian in the woods. He hung around the Canton fire station in order to associate with the horses. He drew them and other forms of life on margins of schoolbooks and in albums. From high school he was sent to a military academy, against which he rebelled, at the same time filling a sketchbook with pictures of cavalrymen battling horseback Indians. At home on vacation, he improvised a studio in an uncle's barn. His models were horses — not only carriage horses but several Western ponies belonging to town people.

In the fall of 1878 he went to Yale University, playing football and studying in the Yale Art School. The one other member of his art class was Poultney Bigelow, who became editor of *Outing* magazine and, in 1886, discovered in some pictures offered him "the real thing, the unspoiled, native genius dealing with Mexican ponies, cowboys, cactus, lariats, and sombreros." The artist turned out to be Remington of Yale.

In 1880, Remington's father died and Frederic inherited a few thousand dollars. He refused to return to Yale but seems not to have known what he wanted until he made a trip to Montana in August of 1881. In 1882, *Harper's Weekly* (February 25) published a picture entitled "Cowboys of Arizona: Roused by a Scout." According to the credit line it was "drawn by W. A. Rogers from a sketch by Frederic Remington."

Young Frederic had been corresponding with a Yale friend named Robert Camp (B.A., 1882) of Milwaukee who had gone to Butler County, Kansas, where he was trying his hand at sheep raising. By the end of 1882 he owned a section of land and 900 sheep. In March, 1883, Remington joined him and bought a quarter section (160 acres) not far from Camp's for $3,400. It had a three-room frame house, a well, a corral, and two barns on it. Shortly thereafter he bought an adjoining quarter section for $1,250. He bought horses before he bought sheep. The one he rode was a dun mare from Texas that would not have been ridden by any self-respecting range man in Texas — solely because she was a mare: such was the etiquette of the times. But she suited Remington and he named her Terra Cotta. He hired a hand named Bill, who by his talk was an authority on horses. They built a sheep shed. Remington then bought several hundred sheep, which Bill left him to herd until he hired a neighboring boy and

177

thus bought his own freedom. He was still chief cook and bottle washer on his own ranch.

At that time sheep were as respectable as mules or cattle. As Robert Taft shows, up to 1885 no conflict in Kansas existed between sheepmen and cowmen. Remington did not become an artist of sheep, though he made a drawing of his own flock. Inside one of his barns he carved on the wooden wall the picture of a cowboy roping a steer. He was depicting the conventional rather than what he saw.

His post office was Peabody, Kansas. Under date of May 11, 1883, he wrote a "legal friend" in Canton, New York: "Papers came all right — are the cheese — man just shot down the street — must go." Robert Taft made full examination of files of Peabody newspapers, interviewed many people, including Robert Camp, Remington's ranching *compadre,* but found no evidence whatsoever of "man just shot down the street." To tell the truth, Remington carried on the shooting most of his life.

Of his practice in drawing during his Kansas sojourn, Robert Taft wrote:

He spent considerable time with his sketch book. He sketched his ranch, his sheep, his neighbors and their activities. He went to Plum Grove and sketched the preacher who visited the schoolhouse on Sundays and the sketch was then passed around the audience. A neighbor bought a trotting horse and Remington drew the horse. Bob Camp's cook was greatly pleased when Remington drew for him on rough wrapping paper a sketch of a cow defending her calf from the attack of a wolf. Many evenings a crowd would gather at the Remington ranch and Remington would sketch the individuals as they "chinned" with one another or as they boxed, for boxing was a favorite sport of the young ranchers. Few cared to put on the gloves with Remington.

In the spring of 1884 he rode horseback to Dodge City, then the "cowboy capital of the world," and other points in the cow country. Back with his sheep, he learned that Terra Cotta could not outdodge a jackrabbit. Then he learned that a mare "looking old and decrepit," owned by a stranger looking still older and more decrepit, could outrun two horses that his friends and his hired man Bill had spent days and nights extolling. He lost Terra Cotta on a bet. He wrote and illustrated the jackrabbit and horse races for *Outing* magazine (New York, May, 1887), under title of "Coursing Rabbits on the Plains."

On Christmas Eve at a schoolhouse party, Remington and his gay friends got so prankish that they were ejected. In a justice of the peace court he paid the costs for his bunch. He did not like dipping sheep, or helping with lambing, or shearing, or any other drudgery. The market for wool was away down before his first clip sold. In May, 1884, after sheep-ranching for two months over a year, he sold out to become a professional artist. Robert Taft points out that his brief ranching experience was essentially contemporaneous with similarly brief ranching experiences of Theodore Roosevelt, Owen Wister, and Emerson Hough. He came to illustrate both Wister and Roosevelt and to know them well. Hough, in sarcasm, later called Buffalo Bill, Ned Buntline, and Frederic Remington "the tripartite" creators of the American West. The Kansas year set him on his course.

In October, 1884, Remington married the girl who had been waiting for him — Eva Caten, of Gloversville, New York, not far from his own home town. They went to Kansas City to live, but Remington's pictures were not finding a buyer and before long Eva returned to the bounteous table of her people, while Frederic rode horseback for Arizona and the Apaches. When he got to New York the next year he found, as has been told, a market in *Outing*, edited by his Yale friend Poultney Bigelow. That same year he broke into *Harper's Weekly*. Eva now joined him in New York and thenceforth they lived together, childless, in reasonable harmony so far as the world knows.

By 1888 he was illustrating Roosevelt's *Ranch Life and the Hunting Trail* and other books and was moving up into the *Century* and other superior magazines. He did a great deal of writing and illustrating for *Harper's Monthly*, beginning in 1889, but did not hit the big pay that *Collier's* provided until 1898. His nonfiction books are made up mostly of materials first used in magazines.

For years after his pictures — with writings — came into demand, Remington alternated pretty much between trips westward for copy, ideas, knowledge, all sorts of notes and sketches and work in his studio. The contents of *Pony Tracks*, both writing and pictures, illustrate the kind of experiences to the West and South that Remington transmuted into what makes him remembered. In December, 1932, at the Piedra Blanca hacienda, in northern Coahuila, Mexico, I encountered an old, stove-up American cowhand who had ridden with Remington across unfenced ranges of that country. He said that nobody had to wait for the stout man, but that he had to have an extra-stout horse under him. A few years later I came to know Montague Stevens, of New Mexico, with whom Remington went on a grizzly hunt that he put into *Harper's Monthly* and later into *Pony Tracks*. General Nelson Miles was on that hunt also, and in his book *Meet Mr. Grizzly* — excellent on hounds, on sense of smell, and on the Trinity College, Cambridge — author Montague Stevens pays a lot more attention to the general than to the artist. The artist in his account pays lively attention to the bear, to hounds and cow horses, and to "a big Texan" who'd been shot by a forty-five, who cooked for the camp and could read sign.

About 1892, Remington bought a house in New Rochelle, not far out of New York City, and established a studio there. In that year, also, he illustrated Parkman's *The Oregon Trail* — one of his outstanding achievements. In 1898 he bought Ingleneuk, a five-acre island in the St. Lawrence River, enlarged the house on it, and built a studio. For another decade, however, New Rochelle was to remain home for the Remingtons.

He could toil terribly, habitually rising at six, breakfasting at seven (half a dozen chops "and other knick knacks" as Mr. Pickwick would say), then working in the studio until midafternoon, often returning in the evening. For a long time he struggled to keep his weight down. At sixteen he described himself as 5 feet 8 inches high, weighing 180 pounds. He was mighty proud of the way he rode up with General Nelson Miles and other seasoned soldiers during their chasing around after Sioux in the year 1890. At that time Remington weighed 215 pounds. In 1894, age thirty-three, he recorded: "Without a drink in three weeks. Did 15 miles a day on foot and am down to 210 pounds." In 1897, age thirty-six, he wrote a friend: "Have been catching trout, killing deer — feel bully — absolutely on the water wagon, but it don't agree with me. I am at 240

pounds and nothing can stop me but an incurable disease."
He had only eleven years left before the incurable disease
would strike him down. Long before the end he had grown
too fleshy to mount a horse or do much walking, but not to
keep on drawing and painting and writing.

In 1894 the sculptor Ruckstull set up a tent on a vacant
lot in New Rochelle, and there other art people of the
community watched him model an equestrian statue for
some military hero, whose name is unimportant, to be
erected in front of the state capitol of Pennsylvania.
Remington was eager to learn the sculptor's technique, and
Ruckstull seems to have been just as eager to teach him.
Augustus Thomas, the playwright whose *Arizona* had
been proposed by Remington, noticed that Remington had
"the sculptor's angle of vision" and encouraged him to
strike out in that field. Here I'm following Helen Card. In
1895, Remington achieved his first and perhaps his best
statue, "The Bronco Buster," which is only two feet high.
In years that followed he achieved twenty-three other
bronzes. Numerous sculptors have made numerous cowboys and range horses but "The Bronco Buster" was the
first in the field. To quote Helen Card again, "Subject was
everything to Remington, and with him techniques and
theories were properly only means to help him tell his
story. . . . Rodin's remark was that if you are unconscious
of the technique, but are moved to the soul [by the result]
then you may be quite certain that the technique is all
there."

In May 1909 the Remingtons moved to an expensive
house and studio on a plot of ground they had bought near
Ridgefield, Connecticut. Remington had burned many pic-

tures with which he was dissatisfied. Although he could not ride horseback in the West any more, he was settling down to put on canvas things that wanted to come out of himself. He had said more than once that he wanted his epitaph to be: HE KNEW THE HORSE. On Christmas Day of that year (1909) he was very ill. The next day he died, forty-eight years, two months, and twenty-six days old.

One cannot be absolute on the numbers, but according to one statement, Remington had completed more than 2,700 paintings and drawings, had illustrated 142 books, and had furnished illustrations for 41 different magazines. He is not being judged now by quantity, and will not be judged by quantity. He knew the horse, all right, and he knew the West — but more as a reporter than as a part of it. At times he was a superb reporter. I would say that in "The Sioux Outbreak in South Dakota," a chapter in *Pony Tracks,* he is a better reporter on cavalrymen than sentimental and loved Ernie Pyle was on American soldiers in World War II.

He knew cavalry horses and cavalrymen better than he knew cows, cow horses, and cowboys. On board a battleship off the Cuban coast during the Spanish-American War, he wrote in an article for *Harper's Weekly*: "I want to hear a shave-tail bawl; I want to get some dust in my throat, kick dewy grass, see a sentry in the moonlight, and talk the language of my tribe."

As well as he pictured and wrote about "my tribe," if what he said in combined mediums be compared with Captain John G. Bourke's *On the Border with Crook,* Remington diminishes in amplitude, in richness of knowledge, in ease and familiarity with land, frontiersmen, soldiers, Indians, and in nobility of outlook.

In the fourteenth edition of the *Encyclopaedia Britannica*, Rembrandt has six pages and Remington has one-sixth of one page. I guess the proportions are about right. Evaluations of Remington will not be right unless the evaluers keep perspective and proportion. Now and then a writer's best, an artist's best — for some imaginers at least — is something untypical, though not unrepresentative — something that has smouldered long in him and is near to him but would hardly be wanted by his rut-following editors, publishers, and public. "The Fight for the Water-hole" is near the climax of Remington's paintings of violence. Placed next to it in a little-known album of reproductions is a picture entitled "A Prayer to the Gray Wolf." It shows an Indian standing with one foot on the head of a dead buffalo partly consumed by wolves while a second Indian stands out on the bleak prairie, maybe ten steps away, his shortened shadow on the ground, arms and hands spread downward, his whole body in an attitude of supplication. He is brother to a wolf trotting around rather near while two of his mates stand away out yonder beyond rifle range. The quietness of everything, the at-oneness between man and beasts (both the quick and the dead) and the earth (including sparse clumps of grass) — this is not the Remington many times iterating "man-just-shot-down-the-street."

It is not necessary to run down good Bourbon in order to enjoy good Scotch, and I trust I am not doing that when I say that Remington toiled too furiously trying to satisfy the demand for naked action to linger and let things soak into him. He knew more than he understood. In this respect he is not the equal of Charles M. Russell, although he may have had some advantage in craftsmanship. I cannot say. As a reporter through eye and ear, through drawing, painting, and writing, Remington habitually got and gave the right words, but less frequently the right tune. Sometimes even his soldiers seem to me clever imitations of Kipling's.

In ripeness, the right tempo is always present. I think of two drawings by Charlie Russell. One of them is "The Trail Boss." He is sidling over in the saddle, resting his knees, while his horse rests on three feet. The two repose on a slight elevation of ground, the herd moseying by, and you may be sure the boss is not looking at the steers in general but in particular. He knows every one in that long, strung-out herd, the drag so far behind that only the dust it raises can be seen. No honest trail boss ever wanted any stampede; but if one should occur in the middle of the night, this boss and the bony cow horse would leap into action — in order to restore quiet.

In my mind's eye I often recall a black-and-white vignette of Russell's, one among forty illustrations he did for *The Virginian*. A cowboy on herd, the fat steers lazily grazing, is prone, asleep, his head in the shade of his horse, the only shade there is. The horse is not used to a man stretched out on the ground under him and is not contented. Russell made "dead man's prices" painting action for calendars and for rich purchasers of Western culture. He also was a sculptor. No bronze he made is more permeated with the beautiful, the spiritual, and with understanding of Indian nature than one called "Secrets of

185

the Night." It is of a medicine man, cunning and mysterious, with an owl, wings spread, beak at the listener's ear.

Well, Frederic Remington reported aright much that nobody can ever again see or hear. If his illustrations for Longfellow's *Hiawatha* are made on somewhat the same principle that an interior decorator chooses pictures, it is to be remembered that he understood the crouch of a panther, the howl of the coyote, and the gesture of the medicine man. If few secrets of the invisible passed into him, he translated the drama of the visible into an astounding variety of pictures that do not fade in interest or power.

Austin, Texas
June 17, 1961

The Gauchos and Horses
of Hudson and Graham

CERTAIN LAND NAMES light my imagination and give me a sense of being in vast spaces: El Llano Estacado (and its brave translation, the Staked Plains), Sierra Madre, Trans-Pecos, Trans-Alpine, the San Augustine Plains (in New Mexico), the Plains of Alberta (in Canada), the Sea of Grass (Conrad Richter's title), the Pampas.

Pampa, in the Quicha Indian tongue of the Argentine, means "space." When World War I ended so long ago, I had a strong inclination to go to the pampas of the Argentine or Venezuela and find a fresh range, a new country for young men such as my father rode into a lifetime ahead of me. I'll never go now. Perhaps it is as well, for since I have never seen how man has tamed them and since all the reading about the pampas I have done or care to do is of the old days when the gauchos — the vaqueros of the South — rode as wild and free and unfenced as the winds that blow between the poles, they remain for me the land of far away and long ago. The pampas — the spaces — seas of grass ruffled into waves by the pampero wind, the vast numbers of varicolored horses and longhorned Spanish cattle as wild as the ostriches, called by the gauchos "Mirth of the Desert." Pampas lonely and immense, and into those spaces of immensity the rawhide-shod gaucho of bolo and knife riding away as unbound as a wedge of loneliness-crying sandhill cranes disappearing into twilight.

In the words of Hudson, written after he had passed his seventy-fifth birthday — in the tight little island: "I am glad to think I shall never revisit them, that I shall finish my life thousands of miles removed from them, cherishing to the end in my heart the image of a beauty that has vanished from the earth."

"Like Paul of Tarsus," Cunninghame Graham wrote, "the Llaneros [the gauchos of Venezuela] were born free. Nature had decreed their freedom. They wanted little, and the little that they did require, nature had placed before them to take with a hide rope and use for their own benefit. All the Llanero wanted was a horse. With him he was free." With this idea of the freedom of spaces always burning inside him, Cunninghame Graham once asked W. H. Hudson: "How many men of cultivation, education, and the rest, have seen the pampa, prairie, desert, or the steppes, and putting off the shackles of their bringing up, stayed there for life and become Indians, Arabs, Cossacks, gauchos; but who ever saw an Indian, Arab, or wild man of any race come of his own accord and put his neck into the noose of sedentary life and end his days a clerk?"

No other English-speakers have pictured the gaucho as W. H. Hudson and Cunninghame Graham have. Nobody at all who has written of American cowboys and Mexican vaqueros has approached Hudson's tales and pictures of the gaucho. Hudson left the pampas when he was thirty-three years old, "put his neck into the noose of a sedentary life" and, while observing and writing of much else in

England, went on remembering *The Purple Land, Far Away and Long Ago, The Birds of La Plata,* making the gaucho people live on in *Tales of the Pampas.* The armadillos, pumas, cattle, horses and other creatures of the pampas he put into the most delightful of all books of its kind, *The Naturalist in La Plata.* Graham went and came. He was a superb horseman and had money for horses. In London's Hyde Park he used to ride Pampa, an Argentine blaze-faced black with sweeping tail that tossed his mane and pawed the earth, "proud of his pride." One day Hudson rose from his seat in the park when Graham rode up, patted the horse, said "Oh, Pampa!" put his arms around his neck and wept. But if Hudson had spent his life on a horse, that life would have faded into nothingness and he would never have left those immortal pictures, lighted by the light of memory, of the long since vanished pampa world.

R. B. Cunninghame Graham belonged to a line of Scots who bled with Wallace. He remembered those forebears. "Memories are the shadows of men's lives." Rememberers of the far past are often regarded by zealots of the present as being unfitted for the future — which the past used to be. To Graham remembering was "natural and human." He sat in Parliament long enough to stir up a riot in Trafalgar Square, to be jailed briefly and stigmatized as a traitor to his class. He disclaimed any interest in empire, in missionaries — other than early Spanish — bent on converting the heathen, or in worldly success. He believed with his rebel friend Wilfrid Scawen Blunt that "the white man's burden, Lord, is the burden of his cash." "Why

189

should we honor the wolves?" he asked. He had enough money, both inherited and earned, to live on and was too civilized to pay out his life in the mere making of more money.

He was only half Scot, the other half Spanish, and he had more sympathy for the Moors, "behaving themselves as if blood circulated in their veins and not sour whey," than for such people as pious Rotarians who regard eating in a noisy restaurant recommended by Duncan Hines as an adventure. He admired vitality and had a contempt for hypocrisy as certified to by the face of a politician, "all spoiled with lines, with puckers around the mouth, a face in which you see all natural passion stultified, and greed writ large and manifest." I can imagine his snorts, were he living now, at the unctuous pratings about "free enterprise" by men who have never known what it is to be free and generous, who have never lifted their heads in one free-spirited laugh, and who have never cared whether other men out of whom they coin their money are free or not. He was a gentleman of honor and spirit and, therefore, a rebel. He upheld the rights of any little country like Morocco or Ireland to "work out its own damnation after the fashion that best pleases it."

Leaving causes and Don Quixote buttings of his head against stone walls aside, he was the representative of the horseback world, often also horseback warfare, from Texas far down into South America. His *Horses of the Conquest* remains a primary book on the Spanish horses of the western continents. In justifying himself for writing the life of Bernal Diaz, chronicler of the *Conquest of Mexico*, he said: "Certain it is that I know little Latin (just as he did). Long years ago I too heard the Indians striking their hands upon their mouths as they came on, swaying like centaurs on their horses and brandishing their spears. I too have shivered by campfires, have known night marches under the southern stars, below Cholechel, in Mexico, in Texas, and in Paraguay. Horses I have owned, especially a little doradillo far down in the grassy pampas. . . ."

This was down in the Rio Plata country, where as a very young man Graham trailed range horses hundreds of miles and learned how to make them swim a wide current. "Grouped together on a little beach of stones, they refused to face the stream. Then, sending out a yoke of oxen to swim first, we pressed on them and made them plunge, and kept dead silence, whilst a naked man upon the other bank called to them and whistled in a minor key; for horses swimming, so the gauchos say, see nothing and head straight for a voice if it calls soothingly." The gauchos considered white horses the best swimmers. If cattle did not like to face the water, they "used to fasten a cow's horns upon the head of a good swimmer, who then plunged into the river and the cattle, seeing the horns, thought it was an animal and followed obediently."

I never had thought of the original meaning of the word "remuda" until Cunninghame Graham taught me. It means "reserve," and that is what the band of saddle horses called a remuda is. What a joy it is after riding on a tired horse to *remudar,* to rope a fresh horse from the *reserve,* saddle him, and ride away with all of his freshness pouring into you!

The gauchos and llaneros that Cunninghame Graham

lived with and lets us live with are like the old vaqueros
in manners, customs, character; their lore is that of the
brush country of Texas and other borderlands. They used
the guaco plant for snakebite; you can buy it in Brownsville
or San Antonio today. When José Antonio Paez, about
whom Graham wrote a biography, was fighting for Vene-
zuelan liberty, his llaneros killed no meat on the march so
that the vultures, those "tracks in the sky," would not
gather on their trail and reveal their presence to the enemy.
Before they made an attack, they got the wind on the
enemy so that when they charged in a gallop the dust
raised by their horses would serve as a smoke screen.

"In those days it was customary to approach any estancia slowly, and still sitting on one's horse, to clap the hands
and at the same time call, 'Ave Maria!' Attracted by the
noise, the owner would come out, and when he was satisfied
that there was no danger, he would say, '*Sin pecado
concebido*' ('Conceived without sin')." Caution and polite-
ness being thus satisfied, the traveler was asked to dis-
mount, to stake out or hobble his horse, and to enter the
kitchen, where he could sit on a horse skull and sip bitter
maté tea and eat meat.

Among gauchos who called R. B. Cunninghame Graham
Don Roberto and who regarded him as *patrón* was a famous *rastreador* — trailer, track-reader. Elsewhere I have
treated of the wonderful art even today exercised by
vaquero trailers of the border country. Like the vaqueros
far to the north and the cowpunchers still on farther north,
the gauchos would sit and draw brands on the ground. One
brand was the "*marca de la flor*" — the fleur-de-lis, "the

flower lily" — once burned on hides from the Laureles Ranch against the Gulf of Mexico to Montana.

The gauchos, says Don Roberto, went barefooted or

wore potro boots, made from the hock-skin of a colt and rendered pliable by frequent rubbing and by grease. Their boots were open at the toes in order that the wearer might catch the stirrup easily when he mounted a wild horse. Their spurs were iron, hammered by a local blacksmith; the rowels measured several inches long, and the whole spur was kept in place by thongs cut from a hide. These spurs, called Nazarenas, the wearers let hang loosely from the heel, and as they walked they clinked upon the stones.

It has been centuries now since the gallants of Elizabethan times delighted to jingle their spurs on the flagstones in Saint Paul's Cathedral. No longer, as in my boyhood, do range riders of North America make their footfalls gay with jinglebobs on their spurs — but is there a braver sound on hard earth than the clank and rattle of spurs? The memory makes me homesick.

The llanero wore a poncho, such as can still be purchased in Saltillo, two blankets sewed together with a hole in the middle. If he did not wear it, he carried it tied behind his saddle. "Thus equipped, with a lazo neatly coiled in front of his right knee and a cow's horn, carved in rude patterns, with crocodiles, horses' and bulls' heads or any other device striking the decorator's fancy, but filled invariably with white rum, the llanero is ready for the road."

Cunninghame Graham liked these men not only because he yearned for free life and fresh air, but because they were interesting "as but the truly ignorant can ever be."

He rode among the Arabs and admired the old sheik who "drank the three cups prescribed by usage, lapping them like a dog, and drawing in his breath like a tired horse at water, to show his great content." I want to sit down with some old rawhide and listen to him blow his coffee, listen to him make a kind of solemn-joyful noise unto the Lord, an unconscious thanksgiving, expressive of the mighty response of his whole body to coffee, while after each gulp he looks as pleased as a dominecker hen on a hot day when she raises her beak to heaven after each bill full of water.

This is a personal essay. The foregoing part of it was written late in 1944 in my black-curtained college room in Cambridge University, where, about dusk every evening, I could hear American and British bombers going over to blast Hitler's Nazis. What I wrote was for a few Texas newspapers that have been publishing my pieces every Sunday since the first one in September, 1939. For a long time the writings of Hudson and Graham had talked to me, and during a year in England I had been collecting their books from the wonderful bookstores of Cambridge, London and other places, meanwhile reading in them — mostly as midnight morsels. A copy of Herbert West's biography of Robert Bontine Cunninghame Graham that I had recently found and devoured, along with Tschiffely's less pleasing *Don Roberto,* rather prompted me to write the foregoing with emphasis on Don Roberto.

By railing against the society to which he belonged, Graham often obstructs one's view of the gaucho he is picturing: he never threw away his Oxford Street shoes to encase his feet in rawhide *botas.* Saying that "only the truly ignorant" can be "interesting" is sheer cant. Perhaps he meant picturesque. He did not wish to be ignorant; he was sophisticated in mind and manners; he wrote to be interesting. He would never have considered even the most "truly ignorant" gaucho more interesting than his friend Hudson, about whom he wrote with understanding. He was vain of his own picturesque appearance, was probably more pleased at being called *singularisimo* by Hudson than with any other adjective ever bestowed upon him. He could reverse the looking glass, however, and called faith, quoting somebody, "that first infirmity of uninstructed minds" — the "truly ignorant." Active-minded vitality is doomed to protest; sometimes Graham was more vital in protest than in picturing the individual as distinguished from the type.

From his brief stories, sketches, histories one may indeed derive a just idea of them, plenteous in detail; for all that, he too often writes *about* the subject. All the horses in Graham's *Horses of the Conquest* added together do not equal in vitality and vividness one unhistoric horse of Hudson's named Cristiano. The facts of life, no matter how arranged, are not life itself. Graham opens a window — his window, in his way — and through it we see a particular gaucho, in a particular place, at a particular time, conducting himself in a manner peculiar to his kind, but he never belonged, intimately and profoundly, to the pampas, to their grasses and Russian thistles, their oven-birds and guanacos, their people as Hudson belonged. Hudson opens a door and the reader instantly passes through it, across a continent, over an ocean, beyond a century of years, to sit down with three gauchos, two women, four children and

195

two maidens on the earthen floor of a hut around a fire on which a pot of mutton boils while the several individuals talk, each in character. Through Hudson's door we are in a tavern, with knifed gauchos, their mounts tied outside, while — never remotely resembling a still-life picture — they talk, act; we are at a cattle-marking where gauchos work — and knife; we are in a night camp where meat alone is eaten and the milk-despising gauchos speak only as meat-eating riders of the spaces, without the slightest conception of any other life, would speak.

Hudson was born on a small *estancia*. He was reared in a house to which came neighboring raisers of livestock and their families; as one belonging to these gaucho people, he rode his horse to visit and linger in their thatched homesteads scattered far between over the unfenced pampas. He spoke and thought in their language, even while becoming familiar with the literature of what he felt to be his homeland. No matter what he wrote about, he wrote out of himself. During his prolonged writing years in England, the gaucho life he had known in his youth, though no longer existing, was more deeply rooted in his memory and in his emotional, imagination-stirred responses than any house, any down, any shepherd, even any bird, of the England that was a loved home to him for almost half a century. Of his books based on England there are few in which some recollection of the pampas does not come up. The pampas remained his *querencia* in the elemental way that a mare of the unfenced *campo* would go back to where she was foaled to have her colt. Perhaps only an earth-man feels this pull, though instinct never dies in even the most machined human being.

Graham rode with the gauchos and llaneros; he understood their tongue; he reported the outsides of them aright; but their homes, their *parientes,* their inner lives he glimpsed only as a visiting stranger. They were to him what cowboys and Indians were to Frederic Remington, who, however authentic as a reporter, always remained an outsider looking in. Furthermore, Graham never approached Hudson in the transporting power of creative imagination.

In *Retrospective Adventures,* Forrest Reid observes that Hudson's human characters, along with horses, sheep and other animals not birds, make one almost regret his lifelong devotion to birds. Hudson had little more use for literalistic ornithologists, no matter how scientific, than he had for women wearing the plumes of market-slaughtered egrets. Yet it may be that no human voice, not even Rima's, ever cried so deep into his heart as the curlew cried. The bird-impassioned few will always care more for what Hudson wrote on birds than for anything else of his. No part of a man can be cut away without effect on what is left. The Hudson of English shepherds and Argentine gauchos is also the Hudson of birds. For some people his *Birds of La Plata* has an intensity of life that *Birds of Town and Village, Birds of London* and other English birds do not have. Everything he wrote of nature is utterly beyond the *pastoral* tradition in literature.

Pictures, pictures! In "El Ombú," one of the supreme short stories of the language, they flow past us, often joyful, like the deep, still waters in some River of Destiny. If *Far Away and Long Ago* is — beyond what is withheld — William Henry Hudson as a boy on the pampas riding

197

wherever birds flew, and at times as free, it is also the speaking vitality of dwellers on and passers over the spaces: the gaucho infidel; Don Gregorio Gandora, who owned three thousand piebald mares, colts and horses and lived in a frenzy to possess more; the Patriarch Don Evaristo living with six wives in one house, to which people from near and far came to benefit from his *remedios;* the beggar on horseback.

[The type] was by no means an uncommon sight in those days when, as the gauchos were accustomed to say, a man without a horse was a man without legs; but it was new to me when one morning I saw a tall man on a tall horse ride up to our gate, accompanied by a boy of nine or ten on a pony. I was struck with the man's singular appearance, sitting upright and stiff in his saddle, staring straight before him. He had long grey hair and beard, and wore a tall straw hat shaped like an inverted flower-pot, with a narrow brim — a form of hat which had lately gone out of fashion among the natives but was still used by a few. Over his clothes he wore a red cloak or poncho, and heavy iron spurs on his feet, which were cased in the *botas de potro,* or long stockings made of a colt's untanned hide.

Arrived at the gate he shouted *Ave Maria purisima* in a loud voice, then proceeded to give an account of himself, informing us that he was a blind man and obliged to subsist on the charity of his neighbours. They in their turn, he said, in providing him with all he required were only doing good to themselves, seeing that those who showed the greatest compassion towards their afflicted fellow-creatures were regarded with special favour by the Powers above.

After delivering himself of all this and much more as if preaching a sermon, he was assisted from his horse and led by the hand to the front door, after which the boy drew back and, folding his arms across his breast, stared haughtily at us children and the others who had congregated at the spot. Evidently he was proud of his position as page or squire or groom of the important person in the tall straw hat, red cloak, and iron spurs, who galloped about the land collecting tribute from the people and talking loftily about the Powers above.

Asked what he required at our hands, the beggar replied that he wanted yerba maté, sugar, bread, and some hard biscuits, also cut tobacco and paper for cigarettes and some leaf tobacco for cigars. When all these things had been given him, he was asked (not ironically) if there was anything else we could supply him with, and he replied, Yes, he was still in want of rice, flour, and farina, an onion or two, a head or two of garlic, also salt, pepper, and pimiento, or red pepper. And when he had received all these comestibles and felt them safely packed in his saddle-bags, he returned thanks, bade goodbye in the most dignified manner, and was led back by the haughty little boy to his tall horse.

Martin Fierro, the epic of gaucho life, initiated what became a cult of the horseback world of South America — a cult less a betrayal to life than the cowboy cult manufactured by Hollywood, pulps and TV. I do not find in *Martin Fierro* pictures equaling some in Hudson's narratives. This from "Niño Diablo" will illustrate.

At this moment a clatter of hoofs, the jangling of a bell, and shouts of a traveller to the horses driven before him, came in at the open door. The dogs roused themselves, almost overturning the children in their hurry to rush out; and up rose Gregory to find out who was approaching with so much noise.

"I know, papita," cried one of the children. "It is Uncle Polycarp."

"You are right, child," said her father. "Cousin Polycarp always arrives at night, shouting to his animals like a troop of Indians." And with that he went out to welcome his boisterous relative.

The traveller soon arrived, spurring his horse, scared at the light and snorting loudly, to within two yards of the door. In a few minutes the saddle was thrown off, the fore feet of the bellmare fettered, and the horse allowed to wander away in quest of pasturage; then the two men turned into the kitchen.

A short, burly man aged about fifty, wearing a soft hat thrust far back on his head, with truculent greenish eyes beneath arched bushy eyebrows, and a thick shapeless nose surmounting a bristly moustache — such was Cousin Polycarp. From neck to feet he was covered with a blue cloth poncho, and on his heels he wore enormous silver spurs that clanked and jangled over the floor like the fetters of a convict. After greeting the women and bestowing the avuncular blessing on the children, who had clamoured for it as for some inestimable boon — he sat down, and flinging back his poncho displayed at his waist a huge silver-hilted knife and a heavy brass-barrelled horse-pistol.

"Heaven be praised for its goodness, Cousin Magdalen," he said. "What with pies and spices your kitchen is more fragrant than a garden of flowers. That's as it should be, for nothing but rum have I tasted this bleak day. And the boys are away fighting, Gregory tells me. Good! When the eaglets have found out their wings let them try their talons. What, Cousin Magdalen, crying for the boys! Would you have had them girls?"

"Yes, a thousand times," she replied, drying her wet eyes on her apron.

"Ah, Magdalen, daughters can't be always young and sweet-tempered, like your brace of pretty partridges yonder. They grow old, Cousin Magdalen — old and ugly and spiteful; and are more bitter and worthless than the wild pumpkin. But I speak not of those who are present, for I would say nothing to offend my respected cousin Ascension, whom may God preserve, though she never married."

"Listen to me, Cousin Polycarp," returned the insulted dame so pointedly alluded to. "Say nothing to me nor of me, and I will also hold my peace concerning you; for you know very well that if I were disposed to open my lips I could say a thousand things."

"Enough, enough, you have already said them a thousand times," he interrupted. "I know all that, cousin; let us say no more."

Mrs. J. Frank Dobie is grateful for permission to reprint the following selections by Mr. Dobie that have been previously published.

"Andy Adams, Cowboy Chronicler." First published in *Southwest Review,* Vol. 11, No. 2, January 1926. Copyright 1926 by *Southwest Review.* Reprinted by permission of the Southern Methodist University Press.

"A Preface on Authentic Liars" from *Tall Tales from Texas,* by Mody C. Boatright. Copyright 1934 by Southwest Press. Reprinted by permission of the Southern Methodist University Press.

"Captain Cook's Place Among Reminiscencers of the West" from *Fifty Years on the Old Frontier as Cowboy, Hunter, Guide, Scout, and Ranchman,* by James H. Cook. New edition copyright © 1957 by the University of Oklahoma Press. Reprinted by permission of the publisher.

"A Summary Introduction to Frederic Remington" from *Pony Tracks,* by Frederic Remington. New edition copyright © 1961 by the University of Oklahoma Press. Reprinted by permission of the publisher.

Foreword to *Sheep, Life on the South Dakota Range,* by Archer B. Gilfillan. Copyright 1928, 1929 by Archer B. Gilfillan. Renewed © 1956, 1957 by Emily Muriel Dean. Reprinted by permission of the University of Minnesota Press and the First Trust Company of Saint Paul.

Preface to *A Treasury of Western Folk-lore,* edited by B. A. Botkin. Copyright © 1951 by B. A. Botkin. Reprinted by permission of Crown Publishers, Inc.

"Charles Siringo, Writer and Man" from *A Texas Cowboy,* by Charles A. Siringo. Copyright 1950 by William Sloane and Company. Reprinted by permission of William Morrow and Company, Inc.

"A Salute to Gene Rhodes" from *The Best Novels and Stories of Eugene Manlove Rhodes,* edited by Frank V. Dearing. Copyright 1949 by Houghton Mifflin Company. Reprinted by permission of W. H. Hutchinson, Literary Executor of the estate of Eugene Manlove Rhodes.

"Belling the Lead Steer" from *Lead Steer and Other Tales,* by Jack Potter. Published by The Leader Press, Clayton, New Mexico. Copyright 1939 by Jack Potter. Reprinted by permission of John S. Otto.

"James Cox and His *Cattle Industry*" from *Historical and Biographical Record of the Cattle Industry and the*

ACKNOWLEDGMENTS

Cattlemen of Texas and Adjacent Territory. Reprint edition © 1960 by the Antiquarian Press Ltd. Reprinted by permission of Sol Lewis, publisher.

Introduction to *Ramona,* by Helen Hunt Jackson. Copyright © 1959 by The Limited Editions Club, Avon, Connecticut, and reprinted by permission.

"The Gauchos and Horses of Hudson and Graham" from *Gauchos of the Pampas and Their Horses* by W. H. Hudson and R. B. Cunninghame Graham. Published in 1963 by Westholm Publications, Hanover, New Hampshire. Reprinted by permission of the publisher.

"Jim Williams and Out Our Way" from *Cowboys Out Our Way,* by James Robert Williams. Copyright 1951 by Charles Scribner's Sons. Reprinted by permission of the publisher.

"Captain John G. Bourke as Soldier, Writer and Man" from *An Apache Campaign in the Sierra Madre,* by John G. Bourke. Copyright © 1958 by Charles Scribner's Sons. Reprinted by permission of the publisher.

Foreword to *Recollections of Early Texas* by John Holland Jenkins. Copyright © 1958 by the University of Texas Press. Reprinted by permission of the publisher.

Introduction to *Home on the Double Bayou* by Ralph Semmes Jackson. Copyright © 1961 by Ralph Semmes

Jackson. Reprinted by permission of the University of Texas Press.

"The Conservatism of Charles M. Russell" from the portfolio *Seven Drawings by Charles M. Russell with an Additional Drawing by Tom Lea*. Copyright 1950 by C. R. Smith. Published by Carl Hertzog. Reprinted by permission of Mr. Hertzog and C. R. Smith.